Soul Purpose

Books by D.E. Tarver

The Warrior Series

The Art of War—Sun Tzu: In Plain English

Book of Five Rings: Miyamoto Musashi

The Hagakure: The Heart of the Warrior

The Code of the Warrior: Budo Shoshinshu

SOUL PURPOSE

❀

The Story of a Modern Day Ronin

D.E. Tarver

Writers Club Press
San Jose New York Lincoln Shanghai

Soul Purpose
The Story of a Modern Day Ronin

All Rights Reserved © 2002 by D E Tarver

No part of this book may be reproduced or transmitted in any form or by any means, graphic, electronic, or mechanical, including photocopying, recording, taping, or by any information storage retrieval system, without the permission in writing from the publisher.

Writers Club Press
an imprint of iUniverse, Inc.

For information address:
iUniverse, Inc.
5220 S. 16th St., Suite 200
Lincoln, NE 68512
www.iuniverse.com

Any resemblance to actual people and events is purely coincidental. This is a work of fiction.

ISBN: 0-595-25005-X

Printed in the United States of America

The Spirit is the Warrior.
—Miyamoto Musashi

CHAPTER 1

❦

December 22, 1961

Roy LeBlanc grabbed the icy brass doorknob and pulled; it did not open. He went on to the next. People wrapped in long overcoats hurried around him breathing like steam locomotives, hands stuffed in pockets, faces red, noses runny. The city of New Orleans looked dull and gray. A biting, misty rain seemed to add the final touch to an already miserable day. Roy couldn't remember a colder one. Except for a few last-minute shoppers, most of the city's people huddled in their homes and snuggled close to whatever source of heat they had, drinking eggnog and singing Christmas carols.

 Roy turned up his jacket collar and shoved his hands deep in his pockets. Smoke-like clouds of steam bellowed from his mouth and nostrils with each breath. He had joined the police force a little over two weeks ago, and wondered if he'd made a bad career choice. At twenty-two, he still had time to go back to school. He thought about it constantly. He'd wanted to help people, make a difference in their lives—not to stand in the freezing rain checking door locks.

 He hurried back to the patrol car, jumped inside, and rubbed his hands together over the heater vents, hoping the warm air might bring a little feeling back to his numb fingers. His reddened face seemed to glow through his naturally brown skin, and his gleaming white smile made him appear as jolly as Santa's chief elf the day after Christmas.

"This is a miserable day," Roy said to Gary Peterson, his partner. "I don't see how those protesters can stand it."

"Freedom Riders?"

"Yeah."

Peterson shook his head slowly. "You've got to admire their courage. I wish them luck."

"Are you going to work the protest?"

"No," Peterson said dryly and offered no further explanation.

"I can't believe you're even working today, this close to Christmas."

Peterson, one of the few black cops on the force, had been there fifteen years and had earned the seniority to take the day off if he wanted, but a lack of family made the holidays more unbearable than working, even under the worse conditions.

"What else am I going to do, sit at the house and watch parades?"

"At least it's warm there."

"I'm warm right here."

"No kidding," Roy said. "You've been sitting in the car all day."

"And you'd feel better if I was at home?" Peterson leaned to the side and passed gas.

"Oh, man! Not again. What have you been eating?"

Peterson burst out laughing like a middle-aged adolescent.

"No wonder your wife left you."

Peterson's face went stone cold, every trace of humor faded. His eyes narrowed and his lips drew tight. "Hey!" he growled. "That's off limits!" He slowly turned his head away from Roy and looked silently out the driver's side window for a few seconds. "I take my farting very seriously."

Roy snickered so hard it almost sounded like a sneeze. "I'm going to get out and check some more doors. Man, you need to see a doctor."

Roy stepped from the car into the cold. He rubbed his hands together then stuffed them in his coat pockets. The cold air burned his throat, and the damp wind seemed to bite through his clothing.

"What's the matter?" Peterson called out. "Don't you think a man has a right to fart when he wants to? It should be included in the Miranda readings. 'You have a right to an attorney. If you cannot afford an attorney, you have the right to shit in your pants.'"

Roy shook his head and chuckled, glad he had drawn Peterson as a partner—at least things never got boring. The NOPD had a policy of matching up rookies with veteran cops to get them accustomed to the streets. The years on the streets seemed to take its toll on most. Some of the salts were so cynical, they were even hard to talk to passing in the hall, much less during an entire shift. Somehow, Peterson had managed to maintain a cheerful personality. Roy checked several more doors, then jumped back in the car to warm himself.

Peterson drove the car slowly for a few yards, easing to a stop at the end of a long alley. December in New Orleans was so unpredictable—either freezing cold, or eighty degrees and sunny. Not a week earlier, when the city teamed with protesters demanding school desegregation, the weather had been fifty degrees warmer without a cloud in the sky. Busloads of protesters had shown up at rallying points on Canal, St. Charles, and Dumane. They had marched up and down the streets waving signs, and singing songs.

Some of the protesters were beaten, and many were arrested, but all in all they held their ground until time to move on to another city. A few remained here and there, waiting for transportation out of town. They kept to themselves, forming tiny communes on the back streets and in abandoned buildings. The cops had rousted some, but left most of them alone until they could leave the city.

Roy opened the door and set one foot on the ground. He rubbed his hands together over the heater vent one last time.

"You know I should stay home, then I wouldn't have to listen to you bellyache about the cold and..."

A tiny whimpering sound drifted through air. "Wait a minute," Roy said, cutting his partner off in mid-joke.

"What?"

"Shhh!"

Roy cocked his head to one side and listened intently for a few seconds. Nothing. He turned to Peterson. "It sounded like crying or something," he said, his brows furrowed. He shoved his head back out the window, squinting his eyes as though it would help him hear better, and peered into the gloomy wet alley. The wind and raindrops splashing against the concrete drowned out any other sound. He was just about to give up when the wind slowed and his ears caught the same faint, thin whimper again. He eased out of the car, trying not to make any sound that might rob him of further clues. A few steps into the alley, he stopped and stood motionless, straining to hear against his own heartbeat.

Peterson came around from his side of the car. "What is it?"

Roy raised one palm back toward him without looking away from the alley. "Just a minute." He took a couple of steps and waited. After a few seconds, he heard another faint cry. "That sounds like a baby!" he said, hoping against his own intuition he was mistaken. He took a few more steps into the cold alley, then stopped and turned his head to keep the wind from blowing in his ears. "There! Did you hear that?"

"I didn't hear anything," Peterson said, yanking up his coat's zipper as far as it would go and puffing out a big billow of steam.

Roy clenched his teeth and closed his eyes for a few seconds to warm them. He held his breath, listening intently. He could not pinpoint the exact origin of the feeble sound. He exhaled slowly, drew in another deep breath and stood still a moment longer. There it was, as clear as it could be—a baby's cry.

His usual bright smile gone, Roy fought the panic rising in his chest and stood wide-eyed, listening. After what seemed like ten minutes he heard it again—a soft crying that grew weaker each time.

He lingered a few more seconds and heard it again, coming from the dumpster a few yards away. Heart pounding, he rushed over and threw open the lid. The stench made him reel back momentarily, but then he was digging through the putrid rubbish frantically, all the while hoping he wouldn't find anything. His mind ran through a million possible explanations-any one of them better than.... A small, bluish tinted foot poked out from under a soggy brown box.

"Oh my God, oh my God!" Roy shouted frantically. He reached inside and pulled out a tiny baby boy. "Oh my God!"

Roy looked into the child's face as he lifted it from the dumpster. It was horribly burned, the face crushed to the point of being caved in. Its nose dangled by a small piece of skin and thick, gooey blood covered his blue-tinted body, and the burned facial skin looked charred around the edges. The umbilical cord, still attached, trailed behind as Roy raised the baby from the dark abyss. He could not have been more than a couple of hours old.

The infant choked and gurgled on its own blood as it struggled for each breath. The infant's cry was no more than a dying whimper. Tears rolled down Roy's face as he tried to cradle the battered child with one hand and wipe at the cold, thick blood with a handkerchief in the other. His skin felt cold to the touch, and Roy was amazed that he'd managed to cling to life as long as he had. Shivering, wet and dying, the child was the most pitiful sight Roy had ever seen. The child's right arm began to convulse as he struggled to draw in another breath.

"He's freezing," Roy said aloud as he hugged the child to his chest with both arms. The boy's arms bounced limply as though death had already claimed him. He let out another weak, gurgled whimper, a plea for life. Roy's chin quivered. Slowly and carefully, he stepped up the alley toward the patrol car. Peterson rushed ahead and called the emergency room.

Roy slid into the seat, holding the infant snugly to his chest and twisting back and forth. "Shhh," he managed, his voice trembling.

"It'll be okay little man. I…" His voice trailed off, drowned by intense anguish and the hot tears streaming down his face. He struggled out of his coat while Peterson hit the siren and gas pedal at the same time. Roy wrapped the jacket around the child and rocked him back and forth. The tot's blood oozed from his open wounds onto Roy's uniform shirt. He turned the heater on full blast.

"Shhh, shhh. It's going to be all right, little man," Roy whispered.

The siren screamed as the squad car sped through the city.

"I can't believe he's still alive," Roy said, clutching the baby close. "He must have been out there for two or three hours." The helpless child continued to cry and choke, each gasp for air sounding like it would be his last. "What kind of people…."

The car screeched to a stop outside the Emergency Room of the New Orleans Charity Hospital. Peterson almost leaped over the hood to open the door. Roy bolted from the car and was met by a young man with a gurney. He reached to take the child, but Roy raced past him in a panic without slowing down.

"I've got him," he shouted over his shoulder.

Before he had gotten far, the young man caught up with him. "Sir, sir, give me the child," he said calmly. "We need to get him into the ER immediately." He placed his hand on Roy's shoulder. "It'll be OK."

Roy stood panting and swallowing for a moment before he carefully passed the quivering infant to the young man and watched them disappear around a corner. He looked down. His hands and shirt were covered with blood. He felt removed, as if everything around him was happening in slow motion. He jumped when Peterson touched his shoulder.

"Calm down buddy, it's going to be okay. Here, why don't you sit over here?" Peterson pointed to a seat next to the wall and gently pushed his partner toward it. "Take a deep breath, man. You look like you're going to pass out."

Roy sucked in air and exhaled sharply.

"There you go. One more time."

Roy took another deep breath. Peterson sat down beside him.

"I just can't believe this. I…" Roy dropped his head into his hands.

Peterson patted Roy's back. "Just relax buddy. I've got the rest of the shift covered. You just hang around here okay?."

Roy nodded. "Thanks."

Peterson sat with him for another half-hour before going back out on patrol. Roy paced up and down the halls of the hospital wringing his hands for what seemed an eternity. He sat down and crossed his legs, then jumped back to his feet and resumed pacing, never once taking his eyes off the door. The hospital smells struck him with a sense of dread and made him grind his teeth. His face twisted into a tight mask of anger, heartache and fear. Finally, the attendant reappeared as suddenly as he had vanished.

"We think he'll be all right, but we'll just have to wait and see. I'm sorry I can't give you a better answer. He's very unstable. If he survives, he'll have severe scars. He has acute hypothermia—he's lucky to be alive."

Roy released the breath he hadn't realized he'd been holding in. "Good," he mumbled, almost to himself.

"Good is right. Good thing you found him when you did. You saved his life."

Roy didn't say anything. His anger and disgust at the whole incident had obliterated any real satisfaction of having saved a life.

"Obviously, we'll have to keep him here for a while," the young man continued. "We get these trash can babies in every couple of weeks, but I've never seen one this bad. His face is really messed up. We repaired it as best we could, but there was a lot a damage. He's going to be horribly scarred, and I'm afraid there's just nothing we can do about it. Like I said, he's lucky to be alive." He didn't look any happier than Roy.

"What about after that?"

The young man shrugged. "After he's better, we'll turn him over to the court. They'll have to decide what happens to him from there." He started to walk away and stopped. "I wouldn't worry," he said. "I'm sure you can check on him whenever you like. You've done a noble thing. Be proud of yourself for it."

"Can I see him?"

"Not today. We have him in a sterile, warm-water bath in a restricted area. Less chance of infection."

Roy nodded. He turned to leave, then stopped. "I'll call later tonight to see how things are going."

"When you do, ask about Billy. That's what we're calling him."

CHAPTER 2

❀

Twenty-nine years later

The Pruit mansion sat in the middle of a twenty-five-acre yard surrounded by majestic, moss-bearing oak trees nearly two-hundred years old. Construction on the old home had ended sixty years before the start of the Civil War, and it had passed from generation to generation ever since. With appropriate updates and expansions having been made along the way, it was just as magnificent today as the day it had been completed. A gardener clipped, trimmed and planted five days a week to keep the lawn immaculate. A lavish water fountain decorated the front yard and sent a shimmering water mist sparkling with rainbow beauty in every direction. Slaves had hand-laid the red brick drive and planted the now huge oak trees that lined the drive on both sides.

Two guards were on duty in the guardhouse at all times to protect the front gate, and two trained watchdogs roamed the yard. A huge iron gate barred entry from the outside world, keeping secret the things that took place behind them. Massive columns lined the front of the three-story house in the old southern style, and a large Olympic pool sparkled in the rear. Two shiny new limousines were parked in the front drive, and two drivers sat in a nearby room waiting for anyone to come out of the house who needed a ride—anyone, that is, except Melissa Pruit, the rightful owner of the property.

The inside of the house looked just as decadent as the outside. Rare and expensive antiques made the mansion look more like a lavish museum than an actual place of dwelling. A huge crystal chandelier, glittering with a million sparkling colors, hung from a gold chain in the middle of the front room. The marble floor lay under expensive, hand-woven rugs, and an extra wide staircase covered with deep, thick carpeting led to the second floor. The smell of furniture polish and floor wax added to the museum persona of the old house.

Upstairs in the study, Melissa Pruit sat in a high-back leather chair that had once belonged to General George Patton. Thick, full lips and perfect teeth made her smile warm and irresistible. Her long thick eyelashes and sparkling crystal blue eyes made her seem as enchanting as Cinderella walking timidly into the crowded ballroom. A petite girl, she appeared as stunningly beautiful and delicate as a petal from an easily bruised flower. Refined, sophisticated, and educated at some of the finest schools in the world, she sparked the desire of every man who encountered her—though none had for quite sometime.

Stephen sat with crossed arms on the edge of a desk given to the family by Napoleon Bonaparte and stared down at the beautiful woman before him, the object of his loathing and fear. He rose to pace back and forth before her.

"What did you think you were going to accomplish?" he growled. At 6′2″, he towered over his child-sized wife.

Melissa flinched with every sound, every movement, but remained silent. Her head tilted toward the floor, her fingers tightly gripping each arm of the chair, she was resolved to face whatever she must. She only hoped her fear did not show on her face.

Staring down at her, Stephen worked the muscles in his jaw until, in a flash of heat and rage, he slapped her across the face as hard as he could. The force of the blow threw her head to one side and sent her sprawling to the floor. "How long are you going to play this game with me, Melissa?"

Gasping, she placed her tiny, trembling hand on the burning cheek and bit her quivering lip. Tears trickled down her face.

Stephen smiled.

"Not again, Stephen, please," she begged.

"Shut up!" he shouted. "I told you what would happen!"

Melissa winced. "Stephen, for God's sake," she quivered.

A quick punch cut her sentence short. Blood trickled down from the corner of her full lips. She lay on the floor sobbing and gasping. She refused to cry aloud, but she could not hold back the steaming tears. Stephen grabbed her chin and turned her face up toward him. "Why don't you give this up, Melissa? You have no proof!" he growled through clenched teeth. He slapped her hard one more time, and spat in her face.

Melissa curled toward the floor, blood dripping from her mouth, tears streaming onto the carpet. She had loved him once; she would have given him anything. Now, he seemed to grow colder and more paranoid every day. He would be happy with nothing less than her last breath, and, at times, even death seemed a better option than what she had. Still, her spirit burned strong within, and she continued day to day, praying for justice.

Born a débutante and christened Melissa Elisabeth Thibodeaux, she had been raised by a family as old and full of pride as Louisiana itself. Ordained to rule over the vast family fortune, she started out with everything a person could want—everything except sight. Never having known sight, she didn't miss it, and had long ago given up hope of ever seeing. Her determination remained in spite of the humiliating and degrading way Stephen had treated her since her father's death.

Stephen reached down, cupped her chin in his strong hand, and turned her delicate face up toward him. "You'd better not get blood on that carpet!" he threatened. "Swallow it!" He jerked her head back and waited while she swallowed the blood in her mouth. "If you ever try to run again I am going to kill you. Do you understand me? I will kill you!"

Melissa nodded as best she could against the force of his grip. He slapped her again, pushed her head forward and wiped the sticky blood on his fingers into her hair. He jerked her head back again. She could do nothing except endure the pain and humiliation. He seemed to feed on her helplessness, and grow stronger with her fear.

"I want a verbal answer," he snarled.

"Yes," she gasped.

Stephen shoved her away. "Now get your pathetic self out of my sight!" he ordered. "And clean your face!"

Melissa scrambled to her feet and started for the door with outstretched hands. She knew his threat of killing her was just that, a threat. If he killed her, he would lose everything; he'd never let that happen. Regardless of what else might take place, she would not die—not until he had found a way to secure the money.

She felt for the doorknob. Her tears had just about stopped, but her face still throbbed from his blows. Blood continued to stream down her throat, but she knew better than to let any drip to the floor. As quietly as possible, she eased the door open.

The phone rang behind her and she stopped. The only phone in the house was Stephen's portable, which he always carried. She knew if she could ever get to it, she might be able to get help, but she also knew the improbability of that ever happening. Still, the ringing sounded like the call of freedom, and always caught her attention. She moved slowly through the door and closed it behind her.

Melissa felt her way down the hall to the sanctuary of her personal quarters, her knees trembling, her heart still racing. Once inside, she felt her way through to the adjoining bathroom, where she leaned over the sink and let the water run over her fingers until it began to warm. The water stung at first when she splashed it on her face, but it was nothing compared to the burning agony and despair that was roaring through her heart like a snarling beast. She wanted to be strong like her father, but couldn't hold her hands back from shaking, or her tiny chin from quivering. Her very soul felt empty, drained of all hope and faith. As her knees buckled and she collapsed on the floor, she buried her bruised face in her hands and wept bitterly.

She wrapped her arms around her knees and cried and rocked until her tiny body had no tears left to shed.

CHAPTER 3

❁

Few tourists ever saw this part of New Orleans. Trash whirled in the wind, piling up against rundown, shabby buildings. Below normal—even for New Orleans. Bums and homeless people lay everywhere, or sat on staircases, or slept on sidewalks among cluttered beer bottles. Apathy permeated the air as thick as greed on the stock-exchange floor. Very few cars were visible, but motorcycles cluttered the roadsides. Old Harley Davidsons lined the curb, parked side-by-side in domino fashion.

A strong smell of urine made the air thick and heavy. There were no Mardi Gras celebrations here, and no holidays; those who inhabited this place were the scum of the earth and did not care. Bikers, ex-cons, druggies, pushers, pimps, and prostitutes formed a regular melting-pot cascade.

The Hot Spot, one of the more popular bars on the street, provided satisfaction for any vice a person could afford, in a matter of minutes. All assortments of drugs and sexual perversions lay but a few dollars away. Ironically, the place had been a cop bar for years, but when the money left the area, so did the duty assignments. Large metal trashcans filled to the top with beer cans now sat on either side of the Hot Spot's front steps, themselves barely visible under the piles of empty containers and bottles. Over the front door, the words "Hot Spot" hung on a small piece of spray-painted plywood. To the uninitiated, the huge door loomed like a portal to utter darkness, a black hole foreboding to anyone who did not belong. Once inside, the eyes needed a few minutes to adjust to the gloom before images would start to take shape.

On a dimly lit stage in the corner, a thin, expressionless girl swayed absently to music coming from an old, outdated jukebox. No one paid any attention to her, but she was the only thing that kept the Hot Spot from being just another dive on the street.

In the opposite corner, two men played eight ball on an old, ragged pool table. The first, a large man with long, matted hair and a thick, shaggy beard, wore a floppy leather hat and oversized black-leather wallet attached to his belt by a dangling silver chain. His dirty T-shirt barely covered his huge potbelly. His vest sported various patches advertising dope, love and peace.

The other man was a bit smaller, but still larger than average. He wore tattered jeans and scuffed-up cowboy boots. He, too, wore a T-shirt, but his hair, although short on top, hung down his neck in back. His right forearm sported a tattoo of the Tasmanian Devil atop a tombstone and the words "Saturday Night's Alright for Fighting" under it. The two had been playing for some time, betting a beer on each game. The smaller man had already won six.

The large man leaned over the table to make a fairly simple shot.

"Eight ball in the corner pocket," he said, pointing with his stick to the designated pocket.

The smaller man started waving his hands over the ball like a magician.

"Whammy, whammy," the man said. "You can't make it now, I put a whammy on it."

The fat man took careful aim, shot and missed. The smaller man moved quickly into place and shot.

"Aaaa, yes!" he shouted. "That's another one."

"I don't think so," the big man fired back. "You up in my face distracting me. I want my shot over!"

"Hey no, no, no you missed!"

"It's your fault, you cheated. You put a whammy on it! That's not right, man." The big man shook his head sadly.

"That's tough, dude. You owe me another beer!"

"No, no," the big man huffed. "You can't just go around putting whammies on people's balls."

The few people in the bar stopped talking and waited to see if there would be a show. James Gunner, the Hot Spot's owner and bartender, watched to see if things were going to get out of hand. Confrontations occurred as commonly as rebel flags at the Hot Spot, and James hesitated calling his bouncer, who had a chip on his shoulder and always seemed to overreact.

The big man moved forward, coming chest-to-neck with his smaller opponent, and shoved him over the table. The smaller man fell on the floor, but sprang quickly to his feet swinging a pool cue like a baseball bat.

Time to put a stop to this, James decided. "Billy!"

The smaller man swung the pool cue at the big man's head. The big man ducked the stick and punched his attacker in the face, knocking his head back and sending blood streaming from his nose. The smaller man touched his nostrils with his fingers and looked at the blood. "That's it, you've really done it now!"

"Billy, get out here and earn your keep!" James yelled.

The door beside the jukebox creaked open. From the darkness of the other room a man stepped out. He stood six feet tall, and weighed over two-hundred pounds. He wore a black T-shirt, jeans, tennis shoes and no belt. His head tilted downward at a forty-five degree angle, and his face bore horrible scars. Charred skin stretched from his forehead to his chin, and what was left of his twisted nose looked caved in. An angry scowl formed his only expression. His eyes stared stone cold, his teeth were clamped together, and his hands were clenched into tight fists. His massive muscular frame moved with the grace and confidence of an angry lion.

He strode directly to the trouble zone, grabbed the bigger man by the hair, pulled him back off-balance, and kicked his feet out from under him. The big man crashed down hard on his back. Billy picked up a pool cue from the table. The smaller man, who had tried to attack the big guy just a few minutes earlier, now came quickly to his defense.

"Leave him alone, you freak!" the small man shouted. "This is none of your bus…"

Billy turned and struck the small man in the forehead with the cue so abruptly it cut him off mid-word. The man staggered. Billy kicked him in the groin. The man doubled over. Then Billy kicked him hard in the face and sent him flying in an arc through the air and onto the floor.

The big man, who had regained his feet, shoved Billy from behind. "Stay out of this, pretty boy!"

Billy turned and walked forward with narrowed eyes and a contemptuous snarl. The big man drew back and took a wild swing at Billy's head. Billy turned with the motion, and grabbed the big man by the back of the neck, sending him head-over-heels onto the floor with a loud thud. Billy stomped on his face, then broke the cue across the edge of the table and placed the razor-sharp point at the big man's throat.

The big man looked into Billy's rage-filled eyes and ceased fighting.

"Hey, man," he gasped, "no big deal, my mistake."

Billy's expression did not change. His fury burned in his hollow eyes.

"Billy!" James ordered. "Calm down, that's enough!"

Billy snarled at the man on the floor, threw the cue to the side and stepped away without ever changing the scowl on his face. He walked straight to the room from which he had come and disappeared into the darkness, slamming the door behind him. He had never spoken a word.

The two bikers scrambled to their feet and made a beeline for the front door. James angrily threw his towel on the bar. The other customers went back to watching the girl, who seemed not to have noticed what had happened.

In the small room, a little lamp hung from the ceiling by its own power cord, providing the room's only source of light. There were no windows and only one door. Martial-arts weapons were strewn about; an old Samurai sword leaned against the wall in the corner. A dirty, tattered cotton mattress lay on the floor across from a torn, ragged chair sitting in the midst of piles of books whose jackets covered dog-eared and highlighted pages. A box filled with several cans of tuna, beans, and other ready-to-eat foods lay beside the mattress on one side, and a loaded weight bench rested in the corner on the other. The room had a musty smell long since lost to its only occupant.

Billy flopped down into the chair. He'd had a hard life. From the time Roy had found him in the trash can, all the way through the orphanage and the years up until this very day, few moments of happiness had found their way to the man with no last name. Roy had tried to adopt him, but the judge had decided that a single cop couldn't provide the proper environment for a young child. Instead of living with the one person who really cared about him, he had been forced into an orphanage with eighty-five other homeless children, who made him the brunt of every cruel prank and snide remark.

Billy had long ago decided that people were not worth the time it took to get to know them. The chip on his shoulder had started during his first infant moments of reasoning and had grown from there. When someone laughed at him, he reacted angrily; after a while, even the slightest look would set him off. He was isolated and alone; he had never kissed a girl, gone on a date, or even hung out with the guys. Loneliness gnawed at him, pursuing him like an evil companion who constantly reminded him of his inferiority. His defensive wall grew taller and stronger by the day until, at last, no one could reach him at all.

Now he sat staring at the floor, unmoving, unblinking, completely disheartened. Billy knew the best he could hope for was a short life. Maybe in the afterlife he would find a way to make sense of his birth. If God were really fair and just, he would have a better life on the other side. There were only so many ticks of the clock he would have to endure. If it weren't the coward's way out, suicide would be more attractive than life, but his pride would not let him accept the weakness, so he filled his time with solitary activities: reading, martial arts, working out, running. They had become not only his pastimes, but his friends. Although loneliness was hard to deal with, solitude gave Billy his only peace. He couldn't handle gawking people who repeatedly looked at him like a monster from an old horror movie.

Billy got out of the chair and walked over to a mirror taped to the wall. He placed one hand on each side and looked at his face. The melted skin looked almost plastic. The grotesque scar twisted across his face like a spider's web, starting in the center at his crooked nose and spread outward in every direction.

"Hello, pretty boy," he said, mocking the biker.

Billy pushed away from the wall and flopped down on the mattress. Clicking off the light, he sat in the darkness, hiding from the pointlessness that was his life.

CHAPTER 4

✤

Roy LeBlanc walked down the sidewalk with a near skip in his step. The beautiful spring day added to his joy. The shining sun, the slight breeze, and the crystal blue sky made him feel energetic and happy, even if he did have to kick trash and old newspapers out of his way.

Roy knew the Hot Spot would be closed at nine o'clock in the morning, but James always let him visit Billy anytime he wanted. He'd talked James into trading Billy's room, board, and meager salary for Billy's services as a bouncer. James hadn't wanted to make the deal at first, but after one of his customers was stabbed to death, he reconsidered. He allowed Billy to sleep in an old storage room and gave him fifty dollars a week for food. Roy had gotten Billy out of jail for beating up customers several times during his first year on the job, but as Billy's reputation among New Orleans' low-life spread, the problems at the bar became fewer. Billy was never booked because all the cops knew him; they'd only hold him until Roy could pick him up.

As a boy, Billy had spent most of his time away from the orphanage in the Eighth District Building on Royal Street, and had been more or less adopted by all the officers at Roy's station. As much as everyone liked him, the other officers deferred to Roy in matters of discipline. When Billy got into trouble, Roy had chewed him out like an angry father. Whenever Billy had needed anything the orphanage did not provide Roy bought it. When Billy needed something Roy could not afford, he collected money from the other officers. Although no official adoption had ever been granted, everyone knew Roy was Billy's self-appointed guardian. They notified Roy in a matter of hours, sometimes minutes, whenever there was any trouble.

Rod didn't particularly like Billy working as a bouncer, but he knew the young man's choices were limited. Billy had quit school in the eighth grade because of his schoolmates' extreme teasing. In spite of his limited formal education, however, he showed quick wit and a rare intelligence. He read extensively, and had a natural understanding for most things. Roy had encouraged him to apply to the police force, but Billy had failed the psychological evaluation. The psychologist had said that because of his turbulent childhood, Billy had a natural tendency toward violence, and in all likelihood, would not be able to maintain control under the pressure of a badge. Based on a battery of tests including the MMPI and Rorschach, Billy was diagnosed with Intermittent Explosive Disorder and Schizoid Personality Disorder which, in English, meant he was a loner with a bad attitude. Roy hated the labels, but knew the doctor had merely told the truth. Billy seemed to go off on people for simply looking at him the wrong way—and God help the person who said something about his face. Billy fought his own self-image, the doctor had explained, to convince himself and others that he had worth, he had value. He longed for acceptance, and until he found it, he would never have any kind of wholeness within.

Roy would think about the doctor's comments every time he came to visit Billy. He so wanted to see him do something more with his life but every time the subject came up, Billy would grow defensive and brush the conversation aside. Roy never failed to bring the matter up however, always hoping that this time he would reach him. Roy walked up the steps and knocked on the door to the bar.

"Yeah, hold on," James shouted from the other side.

Roy stood quietly until the door opened.

"Well, I've been waiting to see you," James said as Roy stepped in to the dark room.

"Why, what did he do?"

"You have got to do something about your boy, man."

"What happened this time?"

"He's roughing up my customers again," snapped James. "I mean, I let him stay in the back and all, as a favor to you, but I don't need this crap."

"Look, I know, and I appreciate it. At least no one's been stabbed lately." He paused to let that sink in before continuing. "Is he here?"

"Of course," James scoffed. "Where else would he be?"

James picked up a case of beer and walked around the bar to stock the cooler. Roy headed toward Billy's door. He had worked hard to find a place for Billy to stay, and he wasn't about to give it up. Billy had not wanted to stay with him, yet he could not hold a job. Sometimes Roy had his hands full just keeping him out of jail. Working at the bar at least kept him off the streets. Roy had no problem calling in old favors to get the job done, and James owed him plenty.

Roy knocked on Billy's door. No response. He knocked again.

"Billy, it's me."

"It's open," a muffled voice called.

Roy opened the creaking door. Billy stood off to one side with his sword in his hand. The dim light from the old pull-cord lamp cast a fuzzy shadow on the far wall, causing Billy's sweaty skin to sparkle. His bulging muscles rippled beneath his tight, smooth skin with each move, his body appeared chiseled out of solid granite—hard, tanned, and muscular. He made one final cut, the blade swishing through the air. He replaced it in its scabbard and leaned it back in the corner.

"Spot me," he said as he moved into position on the weight bench.

Roy moved to the head of the bench and stood ready as Billy lifted the three-hundred-pound weight from its place.

"You had better not drop that thing," Roy said with a hint of pride in his voice, "because I won't be able to handle it."

Billy moved the weight up and down ten times, then began to slow. Eleven became a struggle; on twelve he could not force it up. Roy grabbed hold of the bar and helped set it back into its resting-place. Billy exhaled sharply and sat up. He motioned Roy to take the only other seat in the room.

"Looks like you're getting a good workout."

"It helps a lot when you have someone to spot for you," Billy said, still breathing hard.

"Any time." Roy leaned forward in the chair, placed his elbows on his knees, and clasped his hands together. "Billy, I want to talk to you about the other night."

Billy's countenance instantly changed to a scowl. His eyes narrowed.

"Someone pressing charges again?"

"No, no, it's not that. It's James. He's afraid you're going to hurt someone."

"He asked me to do a job and I'm doing it. Would he rather try it himself?"

Roy raised his hands palms out. "Calm down. No one's trying to attack you here. He just wants you to tone it down a little."

"Those maggots can dish it out but they can't take it," snapped Billy. "Don't I have the right to defend myself?"

"Now, you know full well you're going way beyond defending yourself."

Billy's lips tightened. "Punks," he growled. "They think they can walk all over me, call me names and make fun of me, and I'll just stand there and take it. Fat, lazy maggots! They want to run their mouths, but they don't want to face the consequences. I'm sick of this."

"You can't hate everybody, Billy," Roy insisted. "You never leave this place. It's enough to drive anyone crazy. You need to meet some people."

"I meet people everyday, and conversations like this are the result of it."

"I don't mean here," Roy said, "you need some friends."

"You remember what happened last time?" Billy nearly shouted. "People don't want to be friends, they want someone to laugh at, someone to make them feel better about themselves and their sorry lives!"

"Not everyone is like that," Roy said.

"Yes they are!" Billy insisted. "Every one of them!"

"I'm not."

Billy did not respond. He simply looked down toward the floor.

"Son, I tried to tell you she was…" Roy searched for the right, non-inflammatory word, "not good—at least, for you. But there is someone out there who is the right one. I know there is."

Billy shrugged.

"I know that's why you moved out. And why you stay here in this…" Roy gestured around the room. "…place. You know you could do better, if you wanted to. This is no way to live."

"It suits me," Billy said.

Roy sighed. "You never just go out and have fun."

"What do you want from me?" Billy snapped. "You think I don't know this stinks? You think I don't want a better life? Nobody wants anything to do with me! My own parents tried to kill me! They threw me in the trash." His voice cracked with his rising emotions. He clamped his teeth shut and took in a deep breath through his nostrils.

"It's all right to be upset, Billy."

Billy just shook his head.

Roy knew he wasn't going to get anywhere with this conversation, but he felt he had to try, as always. He walked over to Billy and placed his hand on his shoulder. "Do you need anything?" he softly asked.

Billy shook his head.

"Promise me you will try to take it easy on the customers."

Billy nodded. "I'll try."

"Thank you."

Roy walked toward the door and stopped. "Everything will be fine," he said, not knowing what else to say. He started out.

"I didn't mean to get angry with you," Billy said. "It's just hard for me."

Roy turned around. "I know, son," he said gently. "If you need anything let me know."

Billy nodded. "I will."

Roy dropped his head and left, feeling completely helpless. He told James everything would get better, and again reminded him of Billy's value to the bar. Any glimpse of Billy's personal hell always depressed him, but there was nothing more he could do.

CHAPTER 5

Stephen Pruit sat in his leather chair with his feet propped up on the desk, his hair slicked back, his face closely shaved. He ran his thumb and forefinger down the crease of his twenty-five-hundred dollar suit and absently rubbed one Italian leather shoe against the other. He smoked an expensive Cuban cigar with a lustful decadence, twirling it in his mouth as he puffed, and blew a thin stream of smoke toward the ceiling. Life was good, and he intended to enjoy it.

His brother, Anderson, sat on the opposite side of the desk. Anderson, the pessimist, always got on Stephen's nerves. He could never see the glass as half full, no matter how persuasively anyone pointed it out to him. In Anderson's often-stated opinion, the situation was simply too good to last. If something could go wrong, it would; better safe than sorry; and numerous other clichés seemed to issue forth every time he opened his mouth. Ten years younger than Stephen, Anderson had recently graduated from law school at Tulane University, a gift from Stephen's newly acquired fortune. Anderson had lived in his brother's shadow all his life, more out of fear than admiration. Stephen had always provided for him, but never failed to exact full payment, usually in the same form of humiliation and abuse Melissa now endured. In his dreams, Anderson played the part of hero, rescuing Melissa from his loathsome brother and running away with her—and her millions. Now, under Stephen's bemused glare, he hated himself for his weakness and fear.

"Stephen," Anderson almost whined, "we have to find a way to nail this down."

"You're the lawyer," Stephen said, each word wrapped in a puff of smoke. "You nail it down. There has to be a way to do it. It's just a piece of paper, for Christ's sake."

"Not from where I stand. It's as solid as a bank vault. I haven't been able to find any cracks in it. The old man knew what he was doing. The money stays—no matter what, and if she manages to get away from here, you're done. If anyone else finds out what you're doing, we'll both go to prison. Stephen, lawyers don't do well in prison."

"Sure they do. They were bringing a whole carton last time I checked." Stephen smiled playfully, then took on a more serious tone as Anderson paled to a sickly shade of white. "Well calm down, we're not going to let that happen. I threatened her harshly the other day. She'll stay where she's put."

"You have to do more than just threat."

"Oh really," Stephen smirked, as he brought the cigar up for another puff. "What would you have me do?" He twirled the cigar around with his manicured fingers.

"If she tries to run again, you're going to have to hurt her bad." Anderson swallowed. "Bad enough that she gets the message."

"That's simple for you to say. I don't hate the girl." Stephen puffed the cigar, slowly. "It's not easy, beating a helpless girl. Of course, it's not hard either," he added with a snicker.

"Well, at any rate, until I find a way around this thing, you're going to have to keep her under wraps."

Stephen threw his hands out. "Don't I always?"

Out in the hall, Melissa sat quietly listening to their conversation. She knew Steven would beat her if he caught her, but she had to know what was going on if she was going to have any chance of escaping. Life had become simply unbearable; if she had to risk a thousand beatings, then a thousand it would be.

She heard movement toward the door in the room. She quickly turned away, placed her hand on the wall and began moving along the edge swiftly, sliding her fingers ahead as she went. After only a few steps, she heard the door to the room open and the two men walk out into the hall. She picked up her pace.

"Melissa."

She continued walking, pretending not to hear.

"Melissa!"

She moved a little faster.

"Melissa, stop!"

She stopped abruptly and placed her back against the wall.

"Were you eavesdropping on us?" Stephen's voice was directly in front of her, like a parent who had caught a naughty child with her hand in the cookie jar.

"Oh, no. I would never do that," she said, trying to keep the panic from creeping into her voice.

"Oh really?"

She could smell the cigar in his breath, and feel the heat of it on her cheeks. She turned her face.

"I think you're lying to me, Melissa. What have I told you about lying?"

Melissa shook her head minutely. She did not speak.

"Go to your room, and I'll be there shortly to deal with you."

Melissa's stumbled slowly toward her room, her knees weak, her hands feeling the way along the wall. She could still hear Stephen mumbling behind her. He was showing off to Anderson, she could tell by his smug tone. She reached her room and slipped inside. Stephen had removed the lock on all the doors of the house, except for the ones that led outside.

Melissa sat quietly and waited, knowing it was pointless to try and do anything or go anywhere. After a few minutes, the door opened and closed softly. She trembled at the approach of Stephen's footsteps, then jumped at the first sound of his voice.

"Melissa, honey," he said in a phony soothing voice. "I just don't know what I'm going to do with you. I try to reason with you. I try to talk with you. But all for nothing. You just will not listen."

He touched the top of her head—not the hard, cold touch she felt nine out of ten times. This was far worse, far more gentle. His hand slid down to her cheek and back around behind her neck. He knelt on the bed next to her and pulled her forehead to his.

"It's a shame we have to fight all the time," he whispered.

She squirmed, but his hand clasped the back of her head. He pulled her forward and kissed her. She struggled to turn her face. He grabbed her hair and snatched it back.

"Come on, baby, you're going to hurt my feelings," he said, his voice dripping with lust. He thrust his face into hers and kissed her again, harder, rougher. She clamped her teeth against his tongue. Wrapping himself from behind her, he pulled her back against his chest.

"Melissa!" One hand clutched her breast, the other massaged her groin. "Come on, baby." She pushed at his hands, but her struggling only added to his resolve. He caught her earlobe between his teeth and ground until he could taste blood. "Remember, baby? It's what life's all about, right? The reason you defied your old man so we could get married?" He pushed his thumb into her nipple, his fingers digging into the soft tissue under the arm, his other hand digging through her clothes. "Come on, now, give it to daddy like a good little girl. You know it's what you want. Man and woman as husband and wife, huh?"

Stephen pulled her head back and squeezed her chin. At her cry, he thrust his tongue deep into her mouth and rolled on top of her, tearing at her blouse with his other hand. He was no longer trying to get Melissa to stop struggling. Her whimpering and squirming only made him more excited, more on fire. He caught her wrists as she clawed the air and held them above her head with one hand while he fumbled his pants open with the other and forced her legs open with his knees. He ripped away the last few shred of clothing still in his way. Finally, he slammed into her, the feel of her flesh bursting against his power raising a carnal snarl in his chest and an explosion in his groin.

Melissa lay crumpled on the bed as he had left her, too drained to cry, too battered to move. Her cheeks and chin felt like they'd been in a vise, the side of her head pounded where he had bit her.

Gingerly, she felt at the burning between her legs. An oozing tear made her catch her breath. She rolled onto her side and curled into the fetal position.

"Oh, God," she whispered wearily, "please help me." At length, she groped around for her pillow. Hugging it tightly, she began to rock with the pain. Tears of despair began to slide down her face. "Please, God," she prayed. "Please!"

CHAPTER 6

❁

Billy leaned back against the wall and surveyed his smoky dungeon. The place looked no different than the night before, or the night before that. The night felt no different from any other night in his life, for that matter. He looked over the crowd. Some he had seen there before, and some he had not. The regulars never gave him trouble anymore, but the new people were always starting something, at least the first time. Billy believed in putting trouble away as soon as it began. The longer you let it brew, the bigger the problem would become.

"You give them an inch, then you've got to kick their ass," was his favorite motto, which, more often than not, got him into trouble also. He never wanted to hurt anyone, but he wasn't about to take their insults either. The doctor had told him he fought back against his own self-image, which had grown into a thorny, impenetrable barrier between himself and the rest of the world. He did not know why he'd been born into a life of loneliness and destitution, but he'd long ago decided he would face whatever came his way and continue on.

A haze of cigarette smoke had settled over the room like a London fog. The customers mingled and talked as usual, some loud and drunk, some muttering to themselves, some carrying on sundry types of business that would not be welcome anywhere else. The music's booming, bone-vibrating bass jarred Billy's teeth with every note. The acrid cigarette and beer smell made his stomach queasy.

"Bitch!" Billy looked around the see where the shout had come from. A young black girl jumped to her feet and dashed a beer in the face of one of the men at a near by table. He and the other three men jumped to their feet. One table away, the girl's white boyfriend also jumped up.

"Who do you think you are?" The man shouted at her. "You think you're somebody because you've got this punk with you?"

"Calm down, man," the boyfriend half shouted. "She didn't mean anything by it."

"Shut up, white trash." The man wiped his face with his sleeve as he reached for the knife in his belt with his other hand.

He reached up for the girl, his friends cheering him on. Suddenly, his head jerked back and his feet shot out from under him. He crashed to the floor and looked up. Billy was standing over him. The man abruptly rolled and sprang to his feet.

"Who the hell are you, the Elephant Man?" He squared off against Billy, hunched into attack position and twisted the knife menacingly in his hand. "Looks to me like your face caught on fire, and someone tried to put it out with a wet ax."

The noise of the room ceased. The man's friends slid away, trying to distance themselves from their falling hero. The others in the bar who had previously encountered or even seen a run-in with Billy backed away faster and farther.

"I think it's time for you to leave," Billy snarled. He let his eyes linger on the knife for just a moment, then lifted them to stare deep into the man's widening pupils.

"I still have a full beer," the man said, motioning over to a mug of beer on the table.

Billy looked at the mug and tipped it over with his fingers. "Not anymore. Now leave."

"Who do you think you are?" the man snapped. "Buy me another beer!"

Billy did not answer. The man moved the knife to within an inch of Billy's face.

"I said, you owe me a beer," the man growled through clenched teeth.

Billy did not move, flinch, or show any sign of fear. He had faced this situation so many times before it had almost become part of his daily life.

"Just leave," he said now with a sigh. "I don't want to hurt you."

They stood-off for a long minute, the biker trembling with obvious rage and embarrassment. The only thing on Billy's mind was that if he hurt the guy, James would probably fire him.

"Hey man, let's just go," said one of the other men from the table.

Another long moment passed without a sound. The biker's friend leaned closer to whisper something in his ear. They looked at each other for a second. Finally, the man with the knife swallowed hard. "I don't care who he is, or what he did," he said boldly. "Nobody's going to diss me."

Billy's temper flashed the moment he realized the situation would not end without physical action. In a relaxed move, precise and calm, Billy snatched the knife from the offender's hand, grabbed the back of the man's head and pressed the point against his throat.

"Do you want to die?"

Billy twisted the knife for emphasis. A small trickle of blood ran down the man's neck onto his T-shirt. His heartbeat seemed to echo in the silence. The friend stepped in.

"He didn't mean it, man." He elbowed his buddy. "Did you?"

"No man, I...I didn't mean it."

"He didn't know," the friend interjected.

"No, no, man I didn't know," the offender sputtered.

Billy scowled and lowered the knife. "Leave."

"No problem." The three men scrambled for the door. Halfway there, the offender stopped and turned. "Can I have my knife back?" he asked politely

Billy made no sound. His expression never changed.

"Never mind," the offender said quickly. He wiped the blood from his neck with his fingers. "You keep it."

He bolted out the door.

The girl threw her arms around Billy. "Thanks," she said, pressing her body against him. "My hero." She giggled as she turned her face up toward his.

Billy moved his head quickly to stare at the floor. He could not bring himself to look eye-to-eye with her. He knew he looked hideous. Pretending otherwise was just ridiculous. She reached up and grabbed his chin.

"Billy," she purred. "Look at me. You need to have more confidence. Any girl would be lucky to have you!"

"What about you?" one of the men in the bar shouted across the room.

A look of panic crossed the girl's face.

"I, um…I'm married," she stammered.

"Since when?"

The men laughed. Billy swung his narrowed stare toward the girl, who now looked away. The crowd laughed again, and Billy realized they were scorning him, making him the brunt of yet another joke. He felt torn. Part of him wanted to leave, but a deep-down yearning would not let him break the girl's soft embrace.

"Billy, I can't have a relationship," she said softly. "I'm sorry."

The men in the crowd burst out laughing. Billy pushed the girl back, the muscles in his jaws pulsating as he clenched his fist and turned on the group.

"You people are all the same!" he bellowed.

The laughter trickled away. Billy stomped through the crowd, which quickly parted to let him pass. He flicked his hand and the knife landed on the floor with a loud thud. He faced the crowd again.

"Any one of you are welcome to step forward and laugh in my face," he snarled. No one moved. "That's what I thought."

He strode into his room and slammed the door.

Once inside, he stood in the dark panting and opening and closing his fists, helpless to stop the waves of longing that swept over him. He had waited all his life for someone—someone to be with, someone to love. He didn't care if she were pretty or smart or sophisticated. Just someone to touch him gently, to share the deepest, most intimate part of himself with. He wanted someone to heal the ache in his heart, and to ease the longing of his soul. He had wavered at the girl's and gotten just what he'd always expected: humiliation. That settled it: he would remain a warrior standing alone, dedicated to the principles that he believed in. A rock, unbending, ungiving and uncaring. At least that's what he strove to be. A warrior stands alone, ready to kill, ready to die. He would forge his body to be as deadly as it could be, and stand up for right and good, even if no one else could understand why. It was his freedom, his pride—his only refuge.

Billy flopped down onto the mattress on the floor and rested his back against the wall. He folded his arms across his knees, dropped his head, and waited for the hurricane of mixed emotions that raged inside and twisted together into a knot in his stomach to subside. He knew better than to try facing down the foe that oppressed him. As mighty as his body had become and as strong as his fighting spirit burned, he wouldn't win. He never did. He could not change his circumstances—not until he found the tender acceptance he no longer believed existed for him.

CHAPTER 7

❀

The sun rose on a glorious morning in Metarie, where the Pruit mansion sat secured from the world by a twenty-five-acre fenced yard with countless acres beyond. The sunlight sparkled, the birds sang, and a sundry array of beautiful flowers bloomed. The feel was more like the Garden of Eden than New Orleans. Stephen sat at an elegantly laid-out breakfast, and sipped his coffee with his pinkie in the air.

The morning breeze blew gently across the balcony, carrying the invigorating smells of spring. He looked out over the huge lawn and beautiful water fountain while nibbling on a piece of lightly buttered toast. A butler stood nearby, waiting to take his order for the main course. Stephen put the toast down, unfolded the morning paper, and began to read.

Jay, Chief-of-Security over the house guards, came in, walked quickly to the side of the table and stood patiently awaiting acknowledgment.

After a minute, Stephen looked over the top of his paper. "Good morning, Jay," he said in his most superior sounding voice. "What can I do for you?"

"She's gone, Sir."

Stephen's face went blank, then turned angry. "Well, find her!"

"We have people combing the house now, Sir," Jay said quietly. No matter how angry Stephen got, he knew he would never be fired. Not many good security people would be willing to help him hold Melissa against her will.

"I am about to go search the yard."

Stephen cut the air with his hand "Go, then," he said, as though he expected Jay to vanish in thin air.

Jay left the balcony through the adjoining room, moved quickly down the steps, ambled out of the house and stopped to scan the twelve-foot chain-link fence with razor wire in threatening rings along the top that surrounded the yard. Melissa's father had built the fence to keep people out. Stephen had added the razor wire to keep Melissa in. Jay kept two guards stationed at the front gate at all times to watch the only exit through the fence, which went five feet underground to keep anyone from digging under it, ensuring that she could not get too far even if she did manage to avoid their sight.

The lower part of the yard had quite a few trees. Jay doubted she could have gotten that far, but decided it would be the best place to start looking. At least he would not have to listen to the commotion in the house. He started down the path and his radio squawked.

"I found her," came an excited voice.

"Where?"

"On the south side in the woods."

"What were you doing over there?"

"I heard you guys looking and thought I would lend a hand."

"The next time you hear us looking for something, stay at your post!"

No reply.

"Did you hear that?" Jay demanded.

"Yes, Sir!"

Melissa huddled in a small ravine. She had thought she was well hidden, but though the breeze made it hard, she'd heard the guard's irritated reply. She felt exposed, as if she were laid bare before the world. A chill ran through her body. Panicked, she suddenly leapt to her feet and began stumbling through the underbrush, like a frightened animal running for its life. She had known when she left the house that she probably would not get away, but she had to try, even if the odds were against her.

"Hey! Stop!" She ran faster at the sound of the guard stomping after her. Within seconds someone grabbed her shoulder. She screamed shrilly, twisted away from the grip and slapped wildly. The hands released her and she took off again, only to trip after a few steps and fall face first into the mud. Gasping for air, she scrambled back to her feet and continued to run.

She ran until her outstretched hands slapped against the fence. She had not even known of its existence. She had never been that far from the house except under escort of the chauffeur.

She hurriedly felt her way along the fence, praying for an opening. "It goes all the way around the yard," a voice behind her announced.

By now, Jay had joined the guard, who was patiently watching and waiting. When Melissa started climbing up the links, the security chief moved in. "There's wire across the top," he said, pulling her down by her tiny waist.

Melissa wilted through his arms to the ground. "Please. Please let me go," she pleaded weakly. "You know what he's going to do to me."

"Why didn't you think of that before you tried to run?"

"You know what it's like in there. Please, let me go. Help me. Please." She heard the familiar squawk of his radio.

"I've got her."

Melissa was grabbed by the arm and lifted to her feet. She let her body slump, making Jay have to practically drag her up the hill. When the reached the house, he forced her to stand and walk, leading her up the stairs to the study, where, for some reason, all the beatings took place. By now she had given up hope of rescue or escape, and walked meekly into the study, where she sat quietly, her head and shoulders drooping, her face wet with the tears streaming down.

By the time she heard Stephen walk into the room, she was dry-eyed, subdued and on alert. She could hear the drag of his feet on the carpet as he walked around to stand before her without saying a word. Suddenly, he kicked her under the chin. Her head flew back so sharply she thought he had broken her neck. The chair crashed over backward. Numbness spread through her shoulders and up to the base of her scull. Her body began jerking uncontrollably.

"Stupid!" he screamed. "You knew I would hurt you and you did this anyway!"

The spasms stopped. Melissa rolled onto her stomach and pushed herself dizzily to her knees. Her arms still trembled, and blood poured from her mouth. Stephen stomped on the back of her head. She dropped solidly on the rug. He grabbed a handful of her hair and dragged her off the carpet to the marble part of the floor.

"Why do you push your luck, Melissa?" his voice said from somewhere far away. "You are mine. Whatever I say, you do, or you face the consequences. Do you understand that?"

"Stephen." The word was nothing more than a groan. He again grabbed her by the hair, snatched her to her feet, shoved her against a wall and punched her in the stomach. Her knees buckled, her eyes rolled back in their sockets, and she slid down the wall to the floor, mouth open, gasping for air. He slapped her hard across the face. Blood ran from her mouth and dripped from her chin and she tried desperately to catch her breath. Her face burned where he had slapped her. He dragged her by the hair across the carpet, and lifted her to her feet. He threw open the door and shoved her onto the balcony. She lost her balance and stumbled back as he pushed her against the handrail. He pushed until her feet dangled a few inches off the ground. She felt her weight teeter over the balance point and gurgled a scream, the sensation of falling making her arms flail as she grasped violently for anything stable. She latched onto the handrail.

"I should throw you from here."

He slapped at her grip with something hard, making her fingers ached and her grip loosened.

"No! Wait!"

"Don't try my patience, Melissa," he screamed, shaking her back and forth as though he may let go at anytime.

He jerked her up. Her hand tore away from the handrail. He lifted her tiny form and threw her. She landed against the wall with a thud, slumped to the floor and curled into in a tight ball to protect her midsection. He kicked her on the side of her head, slamming it into the doorframe.

His screams became farther away and more incoherent as they echoed through her head. "I am the boss, Melissa!" he blared. "You do as I say!" With a final stomp on the back of her head, he was gone.

Melissa lay in a pool of her own blood, choking and gasping for each bit of air. She knew she was at the point where she could pick life or death. She had simply to choose one over the other. It was an easy choice; nothing was worth this. This daily torture wasn't life, anyway. She started to let go, and felt herself slipping down, down, down. Suddenly, she saw him, a knight—her knight—readying himself to storm the evil castle and whisk her away to an enchanted world of tender love and absolute safety. A knight so brave, he would lay down his own life for her protection.

She floated away, not to the next life, but into a fantasy world full of chivalry, tenderness and all-enveloping love. She drifted off, perhaps to sleep, perhaps to healing senselessness, with visions of shining armor glittering before her mind's eye.

CHAPTER 8

❈

Stephen sat out by the pool sipping a Margarita and enjoying the afternoon sun. His foot still hurt from where he had kicked Melissa earlier that morning, so he had it soaking in a pan of hot water. He took another drink and looked over the top of the glass at Cyndi, a nineteen-year-old escort and his guest for the evening, playfully splashing about the pool.

Anderson had called a few hours earlier to say he had something vital to discuss. He had met a lawyer who could help with their "problem," as he liked to call it, and thought it urgent enough for them to get together.

"Aren't you going to come in, silly?" asked Cyndi.

"In a bit." He smiled and raised his drink to her.

"Now?" she pleaded.

"In a minute," Stephen said. He preferred to let the excitement build a little more. No rush—he had all the time in the world.

Cyndi pushed her bottom lip out in a mock pout, and dove back underwater. Stephen's will crumbled and he got up and headed for the pool when the intercom from the front gate buzzed. He pressed the button.

"Yeah? What is it?"

"Mr. Anderson Pruit is here to see you, Sir." The guard's voice sounded nasal through the small speaker.

"Let him in," Stephen said, disappointed at the timing. Even millionaires have their problems.

A few minutes later, Anderson came through the patio doors with a big grin on his face.

"I did it," he announced proudly.

"Did what?" Stephen asked, his mind still on the girl in the pool.

"I found a way to get the money." Anderson looked at Cyndi. "I see being a millionaire has its advantages."

Stephen had forgotten all about the girl. "How?"

Anderson remained transfixed on the girl. "Didn't I see her on the cover of Vogue or something."

"Nah, she's just a whore."

"Hey," Cyndi called from the water. "Don't call me that."

"Why?" Stephen snapped. "That's what you are. Now shut up."

"I don't have to take this."

"Really?" Stephen sneered. "Why don't you leave, then?"

Cyndi's brow furrowed and her lips drew tight. She twisted away and paddled silently to the other side of the pool.

"How?" Stephen repeated, slapping Anderson on the arm.

"Oh." Anderson blinked several times before he continued. "Well, the old man said that if anything happened to the girl, all her money would go to charity, right?" Anderson always referred to Melissa as "the girl." It helped him deal with his guilt.

"Yes, and?" Stephen cocked his head to the side and turned his palms upward.

"The old coot never mentioned which charity," Anderson said, a canary cat grin on his face.

"So?" Stephen returned.

"All we have to do is set up a charity and have the girl will her money to it. Once she's gone, we sit back for awhile and suck the money back out of it."

Stephen let the idea rumble through his mind for a moment. "You think this will work?"

"If we get the right people involved, it can't fail."

"Okay. Great." Stephen paused again. "So when do we do it?"

"I met this guy downtown who can set it up. He said for us to take it slow, to let him put the whole thing together, and he'd deliver the money to your front door."

"Isn't that risky? Letting other people get involved? Why don't you just do it?"

"I don't know the right people," Anderson mumbled. "This guy has dinner with the governor. He can pull the right strings. It's going to cost you, though."

"How much?"

"Ten million. But, with this guy making the arrangements, it's a guaranteed success."

Stephen sat back in his chair and took a sip of his drink.

"Well," he drawled, thinking out loud, "that will still leave me eighty." He raised his glass in a toast to Cyndi, still paddling around on the opposite side of the pool. She splashed water at him.

"When can we do it?" he asked.

"The sooner the better. I have to get back and set things up with David." Anderson paused for a moment. "Maybe a week."

"Good deal," Stephen said with finality. "Just let me know when and I'll set up a time for your guy to come out."

"He wants it done at his office, downtown."

"Not a good idea. I don't like taking her away from the house. What if we run into someone she knows? The whole thing could come undone."

"We'll just have to be careful. He wants us to come through the building's main door, introduce ourselves to the receptionist, and make a show of it. He said the more people who see us all go in, the more it looks like it was all her doing. He'll write himself in as her lawyer so if anything should come up later, he can testify that she hired him and even came to his office to sign the paperwork."

"Sounds to me like he wants to cover his own backside. If anything goes wrong, he could support us or dump the whole thing in our laps." Stephen shook his head. "I don't like it. It's too easy for him to hang us out to dry. Besides, a week isn't long enough for her to look presentable to the public. I just had to discipline her again, and I wasn't too careful."

"Well, you've got to admit, it's better than suddenly showing up with a secret eighty-million-dollar will that no one even knew existed. If you ask me that's what would bring the heat down, it looks suspicious. The girl's blind, for heaven's sake! Accidents happen. Besides, this is the only way I can find to do it. It's either this, or let things continue the way they are."

"All right, but I don't like it. I have no choice. Set it up for late next week. We need to give her time to heal some. We don't want to take her in public looking like she's fresh from the combat zone."

Anderson's face became solemn. "Stephen," he said gravely, "In order for this to work, you are going to have to kill her afterwards."

"No problem." Stephen took a deep drink and set his empty glass down with a firm click. "Just set it up."

"All right." Anderson turned to leave. "You got it."

CHAPTER 9

❦

Something felt wrong. She didn't know what, but things seemed amiss. She'd sensed everyone's preoccupation all morning. The radios of the security men had passed her door since before daylight, and she'd awakened to Stephen moving about her room laying out her cloths for the day. He'd treated her unusually kind all morning, so she knew he was up to no good; his kindness always carried a heavy price. He'd mentioned something about taking her to town, which made her uneasy. He'd forbidden her to leave her room for the last week, and never permitted her out of the house at all. Now, a sudden trip into the city—the city, where people milled about in crowds, and police officers stood on every corner. A foreboding lingered in the air and made her skin feel tight.

Melissa heard a knock at the door. "Are you ready?" It was Jay's voice.

She did not answer. She heard the door open and someone—presumably Jay—walk across the room. Her arm was grabbed and she was lifted to her feet and walked to the door.

"Ready," Jay called into the hallway.

"Go ahead and put her in the car," Stephen responded. "I'll be there in just a second."

Melissa's heart beat a little harder than usual in answer to the sickening feeling in the pit of her stomach. Her mind raced through hundreds of possibilities trying to find a suitable explanation for the trip, but none seemed plausible. She hoped he hadn't found a way around the contract. If he had, she was as good as dead.

Jay escorted her down the steps, out through the front door. They stopped and a car door opened. "Careful," he said. A hand pushed on top of her head, guiding her into the car. Melissa slid over to the middle of the seat and sat still, listening. Jay climbed in after her and, the door closed behind him. After what seemed like hours, the car door opened again. "Good morning, dear," Stephen said cheerfully.

He sat on the other side of her. She wiggled between him and Jay. "What's going on, Stephen?"

"Nothing for you to concern yourself with, sweetheart."

Melissa could hear the smile in his voice, and she did not like it. She sat quietly waiting, to hear some clue that might relate to her where events were leading. An ominous feeling taunted her from deep within, and it grew stronger with each unanswered question.

The engine started and the car moved slowly toward the front gate. At the gate, she heard the windows roll down.

"Mrs. Pruit will be joining us this morning," Jay said.

"Yes, sir." A clank, a pause, and the car moved forward slowly again. The window closed. After a few seconds, Melissa felt the gliding, steady movement of the limo. Stephen's phone rang.

"Hello? Ah, good morning. Is everything ready?"

Melissa could hear the sounds of the city now, and knew the constant stopping and starting was from the traffic.

"Good, we'll be there in about twenty minutes…She'll sign; don't worry about that," Stephen said. "Hey, I won't forget this." The phone beeped off. "Melissa dear, we are about to meet a man downtown. He'll have a few papers for you to sign. Then we can get you back home."

"I will not sign anything."

"Yes, you will."

"No, Stephen. I'm not signing anything," she said, her voice tense and determined.

Stephen grabbed her by the hair and jerked her head to the side. "Yes, you will," he returned harshly.

Melissa stiffened. She felt the desperation welling up inside her. Signing those papers would be suicide. Her heart began to pound. She felt an engulfing dread at the thought of reaching their destination.

"Stephen, please." The hopelessness showed in her voice.

"Calm down, dear, this not a big deal," he said, releasing her hair and speaking soothingly. "I just need you to sign a couple of papers."

"It's more than that! I can feel it! Stephen, please!"

Stephen shook her arm. "Calm down," he half shouted, hitting hard on each word. She heard a rapid series of tones distinctive of his phone. "Yeah, I am going to have to bring her up the back way; she's starting to panic."

This is it, Melissa realized. Either I fight now or I give up and die. She began sucking air into her lungs more deeply and rapidly. Like a commission from God, the adrenaline of her fear started pumping through her bloodstream, and her heart began to pound with fierce, chest-shaking beats, surging heavily oxygenated blood through out her body. All the stored glucose in her body shot into her blood, energizing her to the point she shook.

The car came to another stop. She lunged across Jay and grabbed wildly for the door handled. Jay tried to hold her down, and she went wild. Kicking and scratching, biting and screaming, her body writhed in angry, frantic convulsions, she kicked her way free from their hands with everything she had and found the handle. The car started moving again. Melissa flung open the door.

Someone grabbed her wrist. "Stop it, Melissa!" Stephen shouted.

She forced her hand toward her mouth and bit his hand. He screamed and let go, her ankles were being firmly held. She bucked her body, jerking her feet forward and back with as much energy and power her adrenaline-filled body could muster. On the third thrust, she hit Jay in the face and stunned him enough to kick free and pull her self out of the moving car.

Her face slammed against the pavement and stunned her momentarily, but she quickly regained her senses. Staggering to her feet, she ran forward, hands outstretched, hearing cars and honking and shouts of profanities all around.

"Come back here!"

Melissa ran until her feet hit the curb, she stumbled but continued on until her hands felt a brick wall. She began frantically feeling her way down the wall. "Help me, someone! God, please help me!" She shouted as loud as her breathless lungs could manage.

"Calm down now." It was Jay. He grabbed her by the hair. Melissa screamed. Other hands grabbed her from all angles.

"Help me! For God's sake, somebody please help me!" she pleaded, her voice straining.

A hand slapped her hard across her face. "Shut up!" Jay commanded.

"Somebody please, they're going to kill me!" she continued to beg.

Another slap. "Shut up!"

Jay raised his hand to strike again, but an iron fist slammed into the side of his head. The driver and other man from the limo turned to see their boss lying at the feet of a disfigured man with an angry scowl.

"Let her go!" the intruder commanded.

"Butt out of this, freak," the driver warned.

The man slapped him across the face like he was a child. "My name is Billy, and your mouth is about to get you into more trouble than you can get out of!" he warned back.

Melissa sat quietly listening to what was going on. Stephen sat on the edge of his seat watching from across the street.

The driver pulled a gun, but before he could even get it clear of his belt it was in Billy's hand. Billy struck the driver across the head with the barrel, and he crumbled to the ground. Then he pointed the gun at the third man.

"Let her go!" he said growled again.

"Look, man, you're not wanted here," the security guard started.

"Do you want me here, ma'am?" he asked Melissa. She nodded quickly. Stephen jumped out of the car and came running across the street with a knife from the limo bar in his hand.

"Let her go!" Billy said the last man, who still had a grip on Melissa trying to wrestle her back toward the car. Billy shot him in the leg. "Let…her…go!"

The last man quickly released Melissa and fell to the ground. Billy tossed the gun into the sewer. He then kicked the man in the face and sent him sprawling into the path of an oncoming car. The car screeched to a stop only inches from the terrified man's head.

"Learn to pick on someone your own size!"

Having made his way through the traffic, Stephen finally reached Melissa, grabbed her by the shoulder, and brandished the knife, but before he could speak, Billy punched him in the face and snatched her from his grasp. Stephen's face crumpled like a child who had just lost his favorite candy to the school bully.

"Give her back!" he demanded.

"Take her back," came the calm reply.

"Give her back!" Stephen waved the knife to within inches of Billy's face. Billy yawned. Stephen lunged with the knife. Blending with the motion, Billy turned Stephen's hand and forced it to slice the knife across his face. Then he grabbed Stephen's hair and pulled his bleeding face less than an inch away from his own. "Now you look like me."

Stephen grabbed his face with both hands and staggered around until he tripped over Jay and fell. Melissa threw her arms around her savior and clung to him as though he was a mighty oak in the midst of a hurricane. He pulled her closer and walked her quickly around the corner and through the twisting turning back streets of the French Quarter. Finally, he broke the silence.

"Are you okay, Miss?"

Her heart was still pounding, and she was breathing heavily. She nodded quickly. "My name's Melissa," she said, her eyes wide, seeing nothing.

"Do you want me to take you to the hospital?"

"No!"

"Where do you live? Where should I take you?"

"I have no place to go. That was my husband. He was going to kill me." The words came spilling out on top of each other. "He'll find us and…and…" Suddenly, she ran out of breath. She trembled like a small creature hiding from the certain death of a hunter's rifle.

"It's okay. I'll take care of you," he said softly. "Calm down. I'm not going to let anything bad happen to you."

Melissa renewed her grip on Billy's arm and pressed her bruised face next to his strong shoulder a little harder.

CHAPTER 10

❀

Stephen ripped his shirt off and used it to try to stop the blood pouring from the open gash across his face. Traffic on the busy fairway had stopped because of Jay and the other men unconscious or wounded in the street.

Sirens blasted in the distance. Stephen tried to pull himself together and collect his thoughts before the cops arrived. He shook Jay with his foot.

"Get up!" he commanded.

Jay moaned. "What happened?" he slurred.

"Get up. We have to get out of here. We don't need any cops asking what happened. We need to keep a lid on this."

Jay rubbed the side of his head before pushing himself up. "What happened? Wha…Oh man…I thought I was dead…I heard a shot."

"Get these guys to the car," Stephen ordered. "Now!"

Jay wobbled to his feet and started helping the others.

The line of cars slowly began to move again. Jay helped the others into the front seat, got behind the limo wheel and started the big vehicle moving through the intersection. Stephen sat alone in the back, smoldering. How could everything have come undone so quickly? At least he didn't have to talk to the police. He could hardly give them a statement without referring to Melissa, and if they started questioning people, someone would surely mention the girl.

Better to get out of the area with the traffic and find the girl later. No one had seen or heard from Melissa for over a year. If he could keep it that way, there would be a lot fewer questions when she disappeared. A police report with her name on it could put an end to Anderson's carefully arranged plan. He just had to get to her before she could spoil the whole thing. He pulled out his cell phone and dialed.

"We're not going to make it," he said into the mouthpiece. "She got away. Some hero with a twisted face took her. We've got injuries—the kind we don't want reported."

On the other end of the line, David DeBello gave Stephen directions to a doctor who would help without filing the required paperwork for the gunshot wound. Stephen hung up. He raised the privacy screen, removed the folded shirt from his face and tried to get a look at his reflection. He reached up and gently touched the cut. The contact with his unwashed hand made it burn. He jerked his hand away angrily, kicked his foot into the privacy screen and slammed his right hand against the door. Anger exploded in his chest like an erupting volcano, spewing hot molten fury up through his neck that made his face flush and his teeth grind. He kicked at the privacy screen until it shattered into thousands of dark, glittering diamonds.

"You find...." He inhaled deeply once, twice, a third time. "You find him," he shouted to Jay. "You find him and bring him to me. You find him and bring him to me alive, 'cause I'm going to cut him 'til he's nothing but a shred of meat!"

CHAPTER 11

❈

Billy led Melissa up the stairs of the Hot Spot, opened the door, escorted her in, and sat her at the bar where James was busy stocking the cooler with beer for the evening's business.

"Who's this?" James stared pointedly at the cuts on Melissa's face. "What happened?"

"Some guys were trying to beat her up, so I stopped them. I don't know what was going on or why, but she said they were going to kill her. I didn't know where else to bring her."

"Well, if someone's trying to kill her, you shouldn't have brought her here," James said angrily. "Take her to the police!"

"She won't go. She won't even let go of my arm." Billy gently tilted Melissa's face, still etched with terror, upward. James closed the cooler and came around the bar to inspect her.

"Where are you from?" James asked gruffly.

Melissa offered no answer. James passed in front of her. When her eyes did not follow him, his expression changed.

"People are seldom killed for no reason," he said, his voice somewhat softer. "This girl is probably tied up with the mob or something. I can tell by the way she's dressed there's money involved. You'd better get her out of here."

"I thought I would call Roy, and see what he says."

"Well, you get her in the back, out of sight. I'll call Roy."

"You got it." Billy helped Melissa to her feet and led her to his room. She stumbled along beside him, never loosening her grip on his arm. He sat her down on the mattress and carefully lowered himself to sit next to her.

"What's your last name, Melissa?" he asked, quietly marveling at her stunning beauty.

"Pruit." She whispered, afraid someone other than Billy might hear her.

"Melissa, you want to tell me what this is all about?"

"Is has nothing to do with the mob," she said emphatically. "Like I said, the man back there is my husband."

"Yeah, the guy I cut."

"You cut him?" Melissa gasped. "Oh God, he's going to kill you," she said sadly, as though it were inevitable.

Billy smiled. "Well, I doubt it."

"No, you don't know him." she said, resigned now to both their fates.

"Calm down," he said. "Let's lighten the mood."

She shuddered when Billy began to stroke her hair with gentle fingers. After a moment, she forced herself to relax.

"You're very gentle," she whispered, "I'm not use to that."

Billy fondled her hair as though handling a rare and priceless thing of delicate beauty. She began to breath easier. Her body melted into his arms, and she cuddled up next to him. She felt like a baby laying under the protective watch of a mighty archangel with a flaming sword. Billy hugged her close, as an adult would comfort a frightened child, rocking her lightly and caressing her hair and whispering that everything would be all right.

Roy examined the cuts on Melissa's face. "We could get a restraining order," he said.

Melissa shook her head repeatedly. "He murdered my father, I know he did. I don't know how he did it, but he did. And the police can't do anything about it. He'll kill me, too, if he can. Then he'll have everything, …everything!"

"You could file a complaint. We could pick him up and check all this out."

Melissa again shook her head. "I just want to stay here."

"I understand your concern Ma'am, but it's just not a good idea to stay here. It's not safe. Besides, if we're really talking about a murder, it's my duty…"

"The police have been all through this. I already know they can't do anything. Staying here is the safest thing I can do. It's the only place I've felt safe since Daddy died!" Melissa pressed her face next to Billy's shoulder, and clung tightly to his arm.

"Look," Billy joined in, calmer than he'd felt in a long time, "police means paperwork. Paperwork means a paper trail. Leave her here with me and see what you can find out. No one's going to look for her here." He motioned around the room.

"I don't think it's a good idea," Roy repeated. "If she's discovered here, you could find yourself in a really dangerous situation."

"Like I care about that."

Billy cuddled Melissa a little closer. She felt so right in his arms, she responded so perfectly to his embrace, as if her soul was reaching out to touch his and his was reaching right back. For the first time in his life, someone needed him, really needed him. He would not let her down.

"You just do what you can and I'll keep her safe here. What else can we do? She doesn't want to go."

Roy stared at the floor while he weighed the matter in his mind. True, it was very doubtful anyone would look for the girl there. On the other hand, he was a police officer; he had a duty to make a report. Still…"Okay," he said reluctantly at last, "but you both need to stay inside, and keep a low profile. I'm going to worry about you every second I'm not with you. And we need to clean and dress these cuts. I'll be back in a little bit with a First-Aid kit. You guys stay put."

"No problem," Billy said.

Roy left the room, still not convinced he'd made the right decision. This could go so bad, so quickly. He would need to find out as much as he could about Stephen Pruit, ASAP. He stopped at the bar, pulled a small pad out of his pocket, and began jotting down some notes. It was one thing to not trust anyone, but this really was a matter for the police, not for one good-hearted, but emotionally disturbed young man. And he would handpick the officers for the job. Good men, men he could trust. If it came to police protection, he would insure it was the best.

CHAPTER 12

❦

John Sebastion Smith received his training from the finest law enforcement agency in the world, the FBI. He received his bachelor's degree in criminal justice from the University of Georgia, then enlisted for a six-year hitch as a Naval officer. In the Navy, he worked with the Military Police for his first two years, then transferred into military intelligence, where he spent the rest of his time collecting information and doing background checks on Marines assigned to embassy duty. John Smith took to the intelligence field like a prodigy.

He loved the cloak-and-dagger stuff—complete with long trench coats and snubbed-nosed revolvers—and received several letters of commendation, including one from the late President John Fitzgerald Kennedy for his work in the Cuban missile crisis. After the letter from the President, a military review board awarded him a medal for outstanding military service. He had a prefect Service Record Book, and his professional evaluations were always outstanding.

In his last year of active duty, the FBI, CIA and DEA had sent recruiters touting the benefits of joining their individual teams. Although the CIA seemed more closely aligned to his accustomed type of work, John took a liking to the young recruiter from the FBI. They hit it off like long-lost cousins, and before he knew it, John Sebastion Smith was playing outfield for the FBI full time.

After a long and highly successful career with the Bureau, John retired to New Orleans, Louisiana to live out the rest of his life with gusto. The people in New Orleans knew how to have a good time and besides, he had a real weakness for the Creole ladies. He really enjoyed the first year of his retirement. He went to every jazz club in the city with several different lady friends, danced in the streets during Mardi Gras, and drank gallons of Hurricanes at Pat O'Brien's. By the second year, he only drank gallons of Hurricanes at Pat O'Brien's and watched the tourists dance in the streets at Mardi Gras. Sometime into the third year, he'd had enough of retirement and got a desk job with the NOPD as a file clerk.

John had worked there now for six years, and had become the NOPD's information desk. As an unofficial police officer, he fell right back into his old routine of gathering information on various crime figures. He had files that would make J. Edgar Hoover green with envy, and everyone knew if you needed to know anything about anyone in the entire state of Louisiana, you had only to ask John Sebastion Smith. His enthusiasm for his job, and the reverence with which he reminisced about his glorious days with the FBI, soon earned him the nickname G-man.

Roy and G-man had become very good friends over the years. Together, they had put away gallons of Hurricanes at Pat O's while reminiscing about the good old days—when law-enforcement officers could actually do their jobs without the ACLU breathing down their necks. Roy and the G-man definitely came from the same mold, and both carried a heart-felt pride of their lifelong dedication to the pursuit of truth, justice, and the American way.

Now, Roy walked up the steps to the eighth district with the same zeal and righteous indignation he'd had on his first day as a young rookie. He'd determined to find out everything he could about Stephen Pruit, and knew the G-man was the person to talk to. He walked past the front desk with a smile and a wave, and rounded the corner to the open office where twelve desks were shoved next to each other—no partitions, no privacy. No one had any secrets at the eighth district and if they had, they didn't talk about them. At most of the desks, cops were typing out reports with their index fingers.

In the center of the room an overweight man in civilian clothing sporting a big, bushy mustache clicked away at his computer with an expertise none of the others seemed to possess.

"Hey, G-man," Roy called out.

John flashed a big partial-plate grin at his approaching friend. "Howdy, Bub," he returned. He leaned back in his chair, propped his feet on his desk, and interlocked his fingers behind his head. "What can I do you for?"

"There ain't enough money in the world for you to do me!" Roy laughed, extending his hand.

"Nor enough money to pay me to do it, butt-head," John replied. The two shook hands and laughed.

"What is this?" Roy asked, pointing toward the computer.

"Oh, that's mine," John said. "These cheap-os wouldn't buy me one, so I bought it myself."

"So, are you practicing for your career as a computer nerd?"

"Yeah man, I already know how to turn it on, AND off."

Roy chuckled. "Well, I guess the Pentagon's defense computers are safe for the time being." Roy paused. "John, I need some help."

"Of course," he playfully replied. "What do you need?"

"There's this guy I heard about, named Stephen Pruit."

John nodded. "Stephen Pruit," he mumbled.

"I need to know everything I can about him."

John dropped his feet to the floor, turned to his computer and started typing. "Is it S-T-E-V-E-N, or S-T-E-P-H-E-N?"

"S-T-E-P-H-E-N, I think," Roy said. "Try both."

John clicking away at the keyboard. He traced his mustache with his thumb and index finger as he studied the screen. "Stephen Pruit, Stephen Pruit," he mumbled, as he scanned down the list of names. "I don't see a Stephen Pruit. Where's he from?"

"I don't know," Roy admitted. "Just ran across the name yesterday."

"What did he do?"

"Not really sure. Billy showed up with a girl yesterday, and said this guy and his men were beating her up right out in the middle of the street."

"And of course our brave warrior came to her rescue."

"Yeah, and now I'm worried about what he's gotten himself tied up in. The girl won't talk to the police, she won't accept police protection, and she won't leave Billy's side."

"Has she given you any idea what's going on?"

"No, not really, but I think it involves money."

G-man sucked air through his teeth. "That's not good."

"I know. That's why I'm worried. That, and the fact that her father's dead. She says this guy Stephen did it. I haven't had a chance to look it up, but she claims we couldn't—or at least didn't—do anything about it."

"Is it a mob situation? Capparelli maybe?"

"That's what I hope to find out."

"Your boy knows he may be in a lot of danger, right?"

"Well, I tried to tell him, but you know how hardheaded he can be, and the fact that a beautiful girl is hanging on his arm is only making him worse."

"Well, I'll get on it ASAP and let you know as soon as I find something. How is the girl tied to Mr. Pruit?"

"His wife."

"Ouch."

"Yeah, and I'm not sure how to handle it."

"Very carefully, my friend. Don't talk to anyone else until I see what I can find." G-man lowered his voice and leaned closer to Roy. "I have files on six different cops here that I know are dirty. Haven't been able to prove it yet, but they're as dirty as they come. Don't talk to anyone."

Roy nodded. "Who are they?"

"Well, I'm not ready to start pointing them out yet, but as soon as I get enough proof I am going to personally lynch the scum suckers. If you need some help with this in the meantime, check with me, and I'll do you right. Most of the guys around here are squared away, but there are a shit-birds."

"I would feel more comfortable with a posted unit in the area until we know more."

"Done. These guys owe me so many favors I'll never be able to collect them all," John smiled.

"I do appreciate it, Buddy."

"Not a problem. Say, what are you doing later?"

"Nothing really. Why?"

"What say you and me go and have a few?"

"I'd really like to, but I want to get to work on this. I have a few more places to check—old contacts, you know."

"You still have old contacts? Send them to me. I need all of the sources I can get. Besides, I live for this shit."

Roy smiled, "I'll talk to them. If they're willing to talk to you I'll have them give you a call, but you know they're not free."

"Sure they are. If they have their hands on any kind of dirt, they need a friend like me, with friends like mine. I can piss in the right pots, and get shit done."

"You got a point."

Roy left feeling somewhat relieved, yet somewhat more anxious. He stopped to think for a brief moment, then headed for the back streets of the French Quarter.

CHAPTER 13

❦

Like every other night, the New Orleans back streets were full of life, teeming with every sort of creature one could imagine. Pushers, pimps, whores, and tourists roamed the streets with wanderlust unmatched in any other city in the world. The doors to the bars were open, and lively music from several jazz bands drifted into the street at the same time, each competing for its share of the people walking the streets. Criers stood by open barroom doors and practically begged for customers. The signs and pictures in the front windows made promises the law would not allow the bars to keep. What little automobile traffic there was inched its way through the crowded streets, pushing through the sea of pedestrians that rolled around the bumpers like water before a moving ship.

Street performers lined up along Jackson Square. Each had a box, bucket, or hat to entice donations for the entertainment. Within any five-foot section near the open market, tourists could have their portrait painted; buy, barter, or trade for any type of souvenir; pick up any sort of food or drink; catch a horse-drawn buggy ride through the French quarter; or have their fortunes told by a real, live voodoo witch.

From Jackson Square across Royal to Bourbon Street, New Orleans more closely resembled a circus than a city. Each group seldom wandered far from its own territory. The end of Bourbon Street closest to Canal was for the straight crowd, the opposite end was for the gay crowd. It was self-imposed segregation at its finest, and everyone liked it that way. Mid-American tourists, bewildered and terrified after having wandered across the invisible boundary, were common.

The segregated boundary between the tourists and the locals lay just as exact. No one wondered when they'd crossed that line, either. The music faded, the circus disappeared, and the city became enveloped in the darkness of privacy, its streets deserted. With the previous block's upbeat party mood evaporated, the humdrum of dry reality rapidly became the order of the day. Tourists could no longer walk the streets with a drink in their hands, singing and dancing merrily along. The locals would let them know quickly that such behavior belonged on the next block, not here in front of God and everybody.

The Hot Spot was definitely not a tourist attraction. It remained a locals-only establishment, where any first time visitor raised more than a few eyebrows. The mood may have been just as lively, but with a much grainier, real-life texture. No high-gloss, circus excitement here. The people at the Hot Spot were tucked away in their own little ambiguous corner of the world, and they liked it that way.

James was happy with the arrangement, too. He could count on his regulars to provide him with another day's dollar, and that's all he needed. The girls that danced for the customers were just as happy. They could get high every night, have the guys buy them free drinks, and receive the same tips from the same men just like clockwork. Everything was as it had always been at the Hot Spot, except for one small thing. Billy was not standing his usual post—and James did not seem concerned about it.

Billy had managed to free his arm from Melissa's grasp after she fell asleep. Now, he sat between her and the glowing lamp, shielding the light from shining in her face with his body. She was the most beautiful girl he had ever seen, even with the abrasions and scuffs, and he was mesmerized by her delicate features. From the soft bend of her thin little arm, to the curve of her full red lips, she seemed almost doll-like perfect. Her brown hair flowed over her creamy skin, and covered most of her tiny neck. Her hands seemed as small and delicate as rose petals, and she had the most wonderful scent.

It was easy to see she'd grown up accustomed to money, sheltered from the real world. Billy tried to imagine how she had become tied up in her current situation. In some ways, he was thankful she had. It won't last, he told himself firmly. She's too gentle, too beautiful to stay here. I'm the last person on earth who could ever be with someone as perfect as her. But, he allowed himself, I'm going to enjoy every minute until she has to leave. And I'm going to make sure that no one, no one ever hurts her again. Maybe I can't have her, but at least I can protect her. Maybe this was my destiny all along. Thank you, God, for placing her under my protection, if even for a short time. I will not fail in my duty. Of what value is my life, anyway, compared to such a divine creation?

Billy became aware of a rising noise in the bar. Almost immediately, he heard James shout his name. He sprang off the bed and out the door, determined to get whatever needed to be done over as fast as possible.

Melissa woke with a start. She heard strange noises, a crash and a scream of pain, loud music, and angry voices. Her sleep-clouded mind struggled to sort out the barrage of sounds, and she groped for the feel of something familiar, a pillow maybe, or the bedpost. As the sobering clarity of her memory sharpened, fear seized her heart like a rabid pitbull. She reached for the protecting arm that had saved her earlier, and found it not there.

"Billy!" she called out meekly. "Billy? BILLY!"

Her rescuer did not answer. Instead, she heard another loud crash, followed by sounds of scuffling and blaring voices. Oh God, it's Stephen! she thought. He's found me! He's going take me back! Back to the torturous agony. Back to the fear, the loneliness. The beatings! NO! NO! NO! NO! NO! NO!

She fumbled around for something solid until her feet hit a rough surface. She pushed against it until she came to the edge of the bed, and slid over the side, knocking a stack of books over in the process. Using her hands now, she felt along until she got to a corner and could go no further. Curling into a ball, she tried to withdraw into her self, to somehow make herself smaller.

The noise suddenly stopped. A door opened and shut. She began suck one breath quickly on top of another, quietly, hoping against hope she had managed to become invisible, and he wouldn't be able to find her. The footsteps were coming closer, closer. Her heart throbbed against her ribs. Her knuckles ached in the grip of her fist.

"Melissa?" It was Billy's voice.

"Billy! You scared me!"

"Why? What happened?" His voice was closer now, almost on top of her. His hands were on her arms, gently urging her upright, then sliding around to embrace her.

"I thought Stephen had come for me," she said into his chest, tears of relief trickling from the corner of her eyes.

"You don't have to worry about him anymore," Billy said softly.

"You just don't know him."

"I don't have to know him. I know me."

"What do you mean?"

Billy scooped her tiny figure into his powerful arms, and laid her down on the mattress.

"It's just an old philosophy," Billy said, sitting carefully on the edge of the bed and taking her tiny hand in his.

She smiled into the darkness. "Tell me about it."

Billy took a deep breath. Holding her just now, even for those few seconds, had filled him at once with contentment, yearning, and a hundred other emotions he didn't know how to sort out. He commanded his heartbeat to slow down, but it ignored him. He licked his lips, and tried his voice. "An old warrior once said, 'Victory is in the strength of one's self, not in the weakness of the enemy. You should therefore know your strength first, and the enemy's weakness second.'" He swallowed again. "Do you understand?"

"I think so." Melissa's hand found his thigh and snuggled closer. "Please don't leave me."

"I'll try not to, but if I have to go into the other room again, don't be afraid. I'll be right back. No one is going to hurt you. Not anymore."

The sheer confidence in his voice made her believe him. Melissa drifted back to sleep—not the twisting, turning, nightmarish slumber of recent years, but the peaceful rest she hadn't known since before her father died.

Billy sat wrestling with the deluge of strange, frightening, but wonderful emotions that kept flooding over him as he drank in her beauty and kept watch over her slumber for the rest of the night.

CHAPTER 14

❈

David sipped his morning coffee at his favorite restaurant. He set the cup back in its saucer. "I am afraid," David said in a dialect more fake than real, as though he was trying to sound like a refined southern gentleman from an old Civil War movie, "your brother may not be able to finish this deal."

"What do you mean?"

"Well, he's already screwed up. I'm a little afraid to do business with him."

"I'm sure he will get it back on track."

"It's a shame he's going to wind up with so much money, and you're going to be left with nothing," David continued in the same light tone.

"And just what do you mean by *that*?"

"We're sending the money to a charity called 'The Churchill Foundation for the Fainthearted, if you can believe it," David chuckled. "Anyway, it's going through London to Japan, from Japan to Australia, and from Australia to Switzerland. From Switzerland, it'll be sent to eleven different banks around the world to sit until we deem it safe to return it to America. While it's being moved all over, I can route the money to anyone I want—the girl, your brother. Even you."

Anderson ran his finger around the edge of his coffee cup and studied the table. "Are you suggesting that we double-cross my brother?" he asked finally.

"Oh, no, of course not. I'm simply saying it's a shame for you to walk away from this empty-handed. I mean, you've taken just as much risk as he has, yet he's the only one getting paid. That just doesn't sound right to me, that's all." David let a moment pass before he spoke again, this time more quietly. "Beside, I don't trust him."

Anderson licked his lips. "How much would this…extra transaction…cost?"

"Not much. Hardly anything. Only twenty percent."

Anderson turned the idea around a few times. He was no fool. His brother was a sonofabitch, who could easily forget him. On the other hand, he was also a dangerous man—a very dangerous man. "When would you need to know?"

"Not for a few weeks." David interlocked his pudgy little fingers.

"What about Stephen?"

"Let me worry about that."

"Oh man." Anderson exhaled sharply.

"You said he was always pushing you around, right? Talking down to you. Making you agree to things you would ordinarily never think of doing on your own. If we do this, you'll never take any of his guff again."

"Let me consider it," Anderson said.

"If you decide not, we'll simply continue with the original plan. Just let me know."

Anderson nodded slowly.

"When do you see him again?"

Anderson looked at his watch. "Actually, I need to be going now. I'm supposed to already be there."

"I think you should keep our little talk between us."

Anderson grinned. "Yeah, I don't think it would go over well at all."

Anderson thought about the money all the way on the drive out to the mansion. By the time he got there, he'd began to warm to the idea.

"What happened?" he asked as soon as he walked into the office.

"She got away." Stephen said dryly. He was sipping coffee. He kept his head turned so Anderson couldn't see his cheek.

"There were five of you! How could she get away?"

"She floated out the window!" Stephen snapped.

Anderson made a gesture of retreat and sat down across the desk from his brother. The computer screen, turned so both of them could see, displayed a perfect picture of Melissa. Stephen finished punching in her description, and hit the "send" button to digitally fax the photo to his contacts across New Orleans and Baton Rouge, about fifty in all. Then he turned his chair, propped his elbows on the desk and scowled at Anderson. They waited in silence while the computer did its job. Presently, Stephen's portable phone rang.

"So you got it?" Stephen growled. "Well get busy with it." Anderson let his eyes drift around the room. "You're supposed to be the detective," Stephen was saying. "Find her! Just find her…no, find them both!" Stephen snapped the phone closed and tossed it on the desk. It hit the stapler with enough force to send it skimming across the dark wood. Anderson surreptitiously pushed it back from the edge.

"I need to ask you some questions," he said by way of distraction. "Do you want to do it now or later?"

"Yeah, sure, go ahead."

"David wants to know if the cops got involved."

"No."

Anderson pulled a small pad from his pocket to make notes in.

"Was anyone other than our guys hurt? Anyone who might file a report?"

"No."

"Was Melissa or the guy hurt bad enough that they may have gone to the hospital?"

"I don't think so."

"Has anyone, other than myself, come by to question you or talk to you about it?"

"No! Don't you think I would have told you if someone had been here asking questions?" Stephen snarled.

"Look," Anderson almost snapped. "Would you rather do this later?"

"Forget it. Let's do it now and get it over with."

Anderson continued to ask the questions David DeBello was concerned about. David was a powerful man, with close associations to powerful people. If there were any chance of a media scandal, he'd walk away, rather than have his powerful friends distance themselves from him. Without them, he would be powerful no longer.

"Sounds like you handled it right," Anderson said after he ticked off the last question. "We should be able to drop right back into the plan as soon as we get her back. Of course, David will want a cooling-off period to insure that everything is green light."

Stephen nodded slightly, his lips drawn tight and his eyes narrowed. "What do we do if there's a problem?"

"That'll be David's call. Don't worry, though. He'll find a way to get it done, even if it takes a little longer."

"What about the freak who did this?" Stephen turned his head for the first time and pointed the jagged, unstitched gash.

Anderson tried to ignore the surprising sense of satisfaction he got from looking at his brother's wound. "I don't know," he finally said. "Look at it this way: it's a small sacrifice for the amount of money we're talking about."

Stephen grunted, but kept his thoughts, which clearly showed in his face, out of the conversation. "I think once we get her back, we need to ask David to come here," is all he said. "We don't want to risk this again."

"Well," Anderson said, standing up. "I have to get back. Lunch appointment." A trace of smile played on his lips. He walked out of the room and closed the door behind him.

Stephen leaned back in his chair and propped his feet on the desk. He laced his fingers and let his arms drape across his belt line. There remained nothing more he could do at this point. Melissa would turn up eventually, and when she did, he would make no more mistakes.

"Are you hungry? It's about lunch time. I can get whatever you want. Well, fast food, anyway." Billy's voice was on the other side of the room. Melissa had woken this morning to find him still holding her hand.

"I'm starving. Anything will be fine," she added quickly.

"Here, well, I have some tuna, and a few cans of beans."

Melissa crinkled up her nose. "Is that all?" she said before she could stop herself.

"I can get you anything you want. What would you like?"

"I guess a hamburger and fries would be good." Melissa did not like burgers or fast food. Accustomed to meals prepared by a chef, fast food and sweet soda always made her stomach hurt.

"Okay, burgers and fries. Okay."

Melissa heard Billy stride across the floor, felt the whoosh of the door opening and the cut-off of air as it closed. A few seconds later, the door burst open again. "What kind of burger?"

Melissa's brow wrinkled in confusion. "How many kinds are there?"

"Well, you know, McDonalds, Burger King, like that."

"Oh. It really doesn't matter. Get whatever you like best."

"Okay, great. I'll be right back."

Billy strode through the bar toward the exit. He didn't really eat burgers or fast food. They were too expensive and extremely bad for his stomach. He mostly ate bland foods, high in carbohydrates and proteins…Suddenly, he stopped, backtracked, and poked his head through the door again.

"What would you like to drink?"

"Oh, whatever you normally get will be fine."

"Okay."

He closed the door again. She probably wanted a soda. Wasn't that what usually went with fast food? Too sweet for him, but if it made her happy….

James was wiping down the counters. He had a cup of coffee on the bar and several cases of beer on the floor to restock the cooler. He looked up when Billy stopped.

"Since when did you start smiling?"

"I'm just in a good mood."

"A good mood, huh? Well, it's about time."

"James, can I please borrow ten dollars?"

"Please! Since when did you start saying 'please?' What do you want the money for?"

"I want to get Melissa something to eat."

James opened the cash register and handed over a ten-dollar bill. "If she needs anything else, you let me know."

"Will do."

"Has Roy found out anything about her?"

"Haven't heard from him yet," Billy said. "Haven't heard, haven't called." He strode from the room, whistling.

CHAPTER 15

As the garbled, high-pitched tones and static hit computers and fax machines across the state, the machines started piecing together a picture of Melissa, a description of her accomplice, and detailed information on how to pick up an easy $10,000 in reward money. Within minutes, the picture made its rounds and the search was on. By the time the picture was copied and handed out, there were over 600 pictures of Melissa circulating, and as many people looking for her. The bottom half of the entire state, from Baker to Slidell to Opelousas, reeked with hungry bounty hunters looking for a quick paycheck. Their instructions were simple: find her and call the number on the page. Do not approach her or her accomplice—just find their hiding place and call the number.

Tony Masca slid his knobby fingers through his oily hair and pulled his long ponytail over his shoulder. He had worked as a professional "Bail Enforcement Officer" for over ten years and this was the single largest reward he had ever had a chance to collect. He licked his lips, making a slight smacking sound as his tongue slimed across the dry surface.

He preferred the title "Bail Enforcement Officer," to "Bounty Hunter," because he felt it better captured the dignity of his job. After all, he kept the streets free of bail jumpers who had no regard for the law, or for the courts that had granted them bail in the first place.

His old chair creaked as he swiveled back and forth. He wore an old, tired pair of Reeboks, faded jeans, an old T-shirt and a black leather motorcycle jacket, which he felt added to his fierce image. His beard, as such, evidenced nothing more than his abandoning a razor for the last couple of weeks, and his teeth gleamed bright yellow. He squinted his eyes as much as possible, because he felt it made him more intimidating, like Clint Eastwood.

Tony's computer had barely enough RAM to display the picture of Melissa, but after a few slow, labored moments, a photograph appeared on the screen—line by line. He slipped a freshly formatted floppy disk into the appropriate slot and saved the picture. He could take the disk to any local print shop and get as many of any-size photos as he desired.

Less than an hour later he had 100 wallet-size photos, with his name, phone and beeper numbers on the back, to hand out with instructions for anyone who saw the girl to call him, ASAP.

Tony took off from the print shop in his yellow '82 Thunderbird to start the hunt. The cloth interior roof had come unglued over a year ago, and had brushed the top of his head ever since, hanging low enough to make it difficult to see out through the rear-view mirror, and constantly irritating him. If he found the girl, he would get it fixed. He parked in a garage one block off Canal, between Bourbon and Royal, and merged into the French Quarter, not far from where the freak had taken the girl. He walked down Royal, eyeing the various antique shops and art galleries. It seemed strange how Royal catered to the cultured crowd while, one block over, Bourbon catered to the lascivious crowd. Less than 100 yards from one of the world's most expensive art galleries, men dressed up as women and danced for women dressed-up as men.

If a woman can be trapped in a man's body, making the man a homosexual, could a lesbian be trapped in a man's body, making him a heterosexual? Can a homosexual man be trapped in a woman's body? Does the body dictate gender, or does the person's spirit? And if it's the spirit, then from what force does it originate, and can it be slipped into the wrong body like a letter slipped into the wrong mailbox?

Such thoughts occupied Tony's mind every time he came close to Bourbon Street. He tried to think about the questions seriously, as though he was studying a flaw in society's accepted doctrine, but he always became aroused and thought about sex.

Tony approached Jackson Square in a state of near arousal, but quickly snapped back into focus when he saw several pictures of Melissa already floating around. He could see the $10,000 slipping away from him, and he did not like it. Everyone he asked said someone had already talked to them, and yes, if they did see anything, they would call. He knew they were just trying to get rid of him, because they talked as if all the bounty hunters were the same person.

He decided to get away from the crowded area and back into the city where the people lived. Surely, the freak would not be stupid enough to bring the girl to Jackson Square. It had just seemed as good a place to start as any.

Tony headed toward the out-of-the-way areas and started over. He felt much better here—no one had seen the picture yet, and everyone was willing to help. He said the girl had been kidnapped, and he was desperate to find her before the fiend did her harm. Time was of the essence for the girl's survival; anyone with information should to call him immediately. He handed out a picture to everyone along with a description of Billy, the evil phantom who had abducted the innocent young girl. God only knew what he might be doing to her at this very moment.

When he'd passed out all the pictures, he went back to the print shop for more.

Roy pulled a chair over to the desk, picked up a folder, and skimmed through it. Around the room, cops were doing their best to finish all their paperwork before the weekend started. The clickity-clack of old typewriters and buzz of dot-matrix printers made Roy feel at home.

"Anything else?" he asked hopefully.

"That's it. The guy is obviously a shyster, but the only things he's ever been picked up for are all trivial shit like this." G-man snorted his exasperation. "I did, however, talk to some old friends at the Bureau. They finally got back to me this morning with a little more on his state of affairs." G-man smiled, his pride in the FBI evident.

"And…?" Roy prompted

"He married this girl, Melissa Pruit, formerly Melissa Thibodeaux of the New Orleans Thibodeauxes. She comes from old money. A hundred-million-dollars worth of old money—give or take 20 million."

"Man!" Roy sat back, stunned. "I figured she came from a wealthy family, but $100,000,000!"

"This guy, Pruit, met her at Harvard—believe it or not—where he cut the grass. She was born blind and needed help with everything she did. Apparently, he always made himself available to her. One day, evidently to old man Thibodeaux's dismay, the two of them got engaged. The old man came unglued. Filed all kinds of restraining orders, had the guy picked up several times for trespassing and, word is, even talked about having him killed. Daddy remained dead set against the marriage until one day the girl ran away with Pruit, and the only way he could get her back home was to agree to the wedding. But he came up with a prenuptial agreement as thick as a dictionary, covering every aspect of any eventual separation. The girl keeps everything, and Mr. Pruit walks away with exactly what he brought to the marriage: not a single dollar bill. Well, the marriage apparently never was any good. A few years ago, the old man died in an auto accident. All the fingers immediately pointed to Pruit, but nobody could come up with anything hard. It was all circumstantial. The DA wasn't willing to go to bat on this one, so…."

"...so he's been holding her hostage ever since so he won't lose the money."

G-man grimaced. "That's my guess. He's a real bad apple. Nasty man. Dangerous."

"Well, he has certainly done a good job on her. She's convinced he'll kill her if he finds her."

"Unless he's found some way around that contract, I seriously doubt it. According to the contract she has to meet with her lawyer once a year-next month. I'm trying to get more details now, but…."

"But?"

G-man took a deep breath. "You're not going to like this. The day after she got away, her lawyer took one in the head. A car-jacking, supposedly. We'll have hell proving it wasn't. Either way, the lawyer worked alone, so all his cases are tied up until the court can appoint suitable representation for his clients. Melissa Pruit is among the listed."

"Oh, man." Roy dropped his head into his hands. "Billy said she was screaming they were going to kill her when he found them."

"The lady may be blind, but I think she can see the writing on the wall. Sounds like he stumbled into something really bad. You know, he's playing out of his league."

"I know it," Roy mumbled, never taking his eyes off the floor.

"What are you going to do?"

"I'm not sure. The girl is completely uncooperative with me. She's latched onto Billy like he's her last best hope."

"What does that mean, 'last best hope?'"

"Hell, I don't know. Something I always hear from politicians. Just sounded like the right thing to say." Roy sat for a moment, then shook his head. "Anyway, I know Billy is not going to let her go, especially if she wants to stay."

"You need to show him that protection is best for the girl's own safety."

"He's convinced he can protect her better, and both of them believe Stephen has about half the police force in his back pocket."

"Like I said, we can handpick the men, keep the information quiet. You need to remind him this is real life, and not some cheap samurai movie."

Roy grinned. "Why don't you tell him?"

"Oh no. Not me," G-man put his hands up. "He's your responsibility."

"Yeah, that's what I thought," Roy chuckled. "Everybody's got advice, but nobody wants to carry it out."

"As I remember, that bastard's about half crazy."

"He's more than half crazy with this girl on his arm," Roy said. "He's acting like King Kong climbing the Empire State Building."

"King Kong fell off of the building and died."

"I know."

CHAPTER 16

❀

The early morning light slowly made its way over the Mississippi River, across the top of the Superdome, and flooded the Big Easy with a soft, hazy glow. The Crescent City came alive with people on their way to pay for their two-point-five kids and a dog, the American Dream seemingly more illusion than reality once the hustle was in full swing.

No sunlight brightened Billy's little room. Only the large trucks dumping the trash bins out in the alley provided a hint of morning's arrival. Billy had awakened several hours earlier, made a pot of coffee in the bar, and now sipped on a cup as he tried to read a book. Every so often, he looked up. The lamp light cast an angelic glow over Melissa's face, like a halo, and he found it difficult to concentrate on anything else.

Angel Face, Billy thought. His heart stirred in his chest against his will, a mixture of unfamiliar yet wonderful yearnings and happiness overwhelming him. How could anyone who considered himself a man strike such a delicate thing? He laid the open book across his chest, cradled his cup, and drank in her loveliness. This might be the closest he would ever come to real happiness, and he wanted to get as much of it as he could before she had to leave, and he returned to his dismal, lonely existence. He knew in his heart he'd pay for this avalanche of feelings later. Still, he could not fight them. They overpowered his every thought, his every intuition and instinct. Billy had finally met his match in this tiny, delicate woman.

His thoughts terrified him, because he knew the overwhelming power to which he was becoming enslaved would not—could not—be returned. A creature so heavenly could but loathe a hideous thing like himself. For the first time in a long while, Billy felt like a freak. He swallowed a lump in his throat and took a deep breath. He needed to get a handle on himself. The world's greatest crime is love unrequited. He desperately wanted to avoid being its victim again.

Melissa moved a little. Billy instantly shifted to the edge of his seat, but she settled back into her dream world and lay still. He relaxed. After an entire life learning not to care about people, his only concern now was to bring her the slightest pleasure—a strange feeling, but he was helpless to do anything about it. In just a few short hours, he had become her prisoner. Watching her, unable to take his eyes off her, he made the conscious decision to glean as much pleasure with her as possible before she was snatched from his life. He already knew how much it would hurt when she was gone. He'd just have to face that later.

"Billy?"

Instantly jarred from his trance, he answered softly. "I'm right here."

"I woke up and couldn't find you." Melissa sighed. "I guess I'm just being paranoid."

"I can certainly understand why, but you don't have to worry now. You can just let all that fade away. I'm here. I'll protect you." Billy's voice resounded, strong, unwavering, lovingly warm.

Melissa smiled and stretched like a contented cat.

"Would you like a cup of coffee?" he asked.

"Do you have tea? Earl Grey?"

"I'm afraid not. Around here it's coffee or beer."

"Coffee then. I can't stand beer."

"How do you like it?"

"One sugar, one cream."

"Okay. Hold on just a sec."

Billy jumped to his feet and left the room. After a few moments, he returned with a cup of coffee and a few packets of sugar and cream. He gently lifted one of her hands and set the cup in it, making sure she had a good grip on the handle before he softly released her fingers. She tasted the hot liquid and made a sour face.

"I brought a couple of extra sugars and creams, in case you wanted more."

"Thank you. A bit more sugar, I think." Her smile made his knees weak. He sat down carefully next to her.

"Hold on, I'll fix it for you." Billy ripped the top off one of the sugars. He cupped his hand around hers to hold the mug steady as he poured and stirred.

"Thank you," she repeated, as she lifted the cup to her lips. She took a drink. "Oh my!" she gasped, as though she had lost her breath. She leaned over to set the cup on the floor.

"More sugar?"

"I don't think sugar is going to help that stuff."

"What is it?"

"I don't know, but it's hard to believe it's coffee."

A big smile crossed Billy's face. She looked so cute with her face all crunched up and her nose crinkled as though fighting off a horrid odor. "It is pretty strong. I make it that way on purpose. It wakes me up."

"Oh! I'm sure it does. I think maybe I'd rather have the beer."

"I thought you don't like beer," Billy chuckled.

"Anything is better than that. I've got to get this taste out of my mouth."

"You know what? I just remembered—we might have some soda. James uses it for mixed drinks."

"That would be great."

Billy rushed out to the bar and returned shortly with a small glass of soda. "Here you go," he said, once again enjoying the luxury of cuddling her hand until she had a firm grip on the glass.

She quickly drank half the glass. "Thank you," she whispered, sighing as though relieved from the foul taste of the coffee.

"You're welcome," Billy beamed, his smile bright and glowing.

"Why are you smiling?"

"How did you know I'm smiling?"

"I can hear it in your voice."

"I just thought you looked so cute with your little angel face all crunched up."

"Oh!"

Billy realized what he had said, and his heart dropped to his feet. Even with an iron will and the discipline of a Marine, he could not keep his bounding emotion from seeping out.

"Sorry," he murmured.

"For what?" Melissa asked. "For taking such good care of me?" She felt for his arm, pulled him down to sit next to her again, and laid her head on his shoulder.

Billy began to tremble. "I will take care of you with every last bit of strength I have," he vowed. He could not believe this angel was actually holding him. HIM, the person who had never even had a friend, or ever dared entertain such a lofty fantasy as this. His resolve grew stronger than ever—whatever else happened on the face of the planet earth, as long as he lived, she would remain safe.

Melissa heard Billy's heart pounding in her ear, felt its strength pumping against her cheek. They sat there together, their silence filling the room, their unspoken passions flowing back and forth between them. His were timid but intense, so different from what she'd felt with Stephen even at the beginning of their marriage. They came, she realized with a shock, from the depths of Billy's heart. A solitary tear of joy and gratitude trickled down onto her smiling lips.

She pulled his arm around her shoulder, snuggled closer, and softly lay her head on his heaving chest.

"Thank you," was all she could whisper.

CHAPTER 17

Tony Masca practically lived on the French Quarter streets for three days after receiving the fax. He had handed out all his original snapshots the first day, and had replenished his stock three times. Tony passed out the photos and tried to describe the freak's face to everyone he met. He hung out in bars, talked to people on the street, sat around with bums, and even offered small sums of money for information leading to the capture of his prey. Wandering the streets, he did without bed or personal hygiene—no big deal to him anyway. Tony was determined to collect the $10,000.00 reward. He wanted that money. He needed that money. He would have that money.

He was working the crowd outside a supermarket on the third afternoon when he finally received his first break. A huge fat lady waddled slowly out of the store propped up on a shopping cart. She pushed the cart, took a step, pushed the cart, took a step.

Tony held Melissa's photo before the woman's large round face. She continued to shuffle forward until the paper touched her face, then folded and slid around her cheek. She continued forward without saying a word.

"Excuse me ma'am."

"What?" The word came out in a gasp of breath.

"I was just wondering if, maybe, you have seen this girl?"

"No." She pushed the cart.

Tony moved to her side. "She's been kidnapped."

"Okay."

"It's very important we find her as soon as possible. She may be in grave danger."

The woman nodded as she sucked in a deep breath and exhaled.

"What about a man with a really messed-up face—big guy, maybe 210 pounds or so?"

The woman looked at him for the first time.

"You've seen him?" Tony asked excitedly.

She leaned over the shopping cart huffing and puffing. "I—I think, woof, I think so." She wiped her brow with the back of her hand.

"Really? Where, when?"

The woman raised her hand and gasped a few deep breaths. "Here. Shops here sometimes, I think. Doesn't buy much. Comes sometimes."

"When was the last time you saw him?"

"Don't remember." She started shuffling forward again. "Got to go. Ice cream."

Tony jumped in front of the cart. "When?"

"Few days, maybe. Look, I got ice cream. It's melting."

"But this girl may be in danger." He held up the picture of Melissa.

"Don't know the girl." She pointed a finger at his face. "My ice cream is melting. Move or I'll run you over." She shoved the cart forward.

After questioning several of the cashiers at the store, Tony felt confident the freak indeed shopped there from time to time. Within ten minutes, he had moved his Thunderbird to the parking lot and set up watch. The store didn't close until midnight, and opened again at five a.m. That would give him roughly four hours to sleep after deducting driving time.

Less than an hour after he'd set up surveillance, Tony's clothes were soaked with sweat. A slight breeze occasionally seldom drifted through the windows providing a little solace from the deep-afternoon heat. He never thought of leaving, though. Hurry up and wait was the nature of his job. He spent the rest of the day sitting in his car smoking one cigarette after another and watching the people come and go. He especially liked watching the pretty girls. Every one of them had their own life splintering off in a different direction. Each person seemed wrapped in an invisible cocoon containing all of the things familiar to them: their friends, their relatives, their favorite television shows, everything that made them who they were tucked safely inside.

Tony had spent years learning and exploiting what he called the realities of people's natures, and had developed his own philosophy of life along the way. Most people, he knew, cared strongly for their own loved ones, but had little regard for anyone else's. From where does a person's value come if not from his loved ones? If it is from his loved ones, then it's not real value, but perceived value. Therefore, a person's value related directly to the extent that his family and friends cared for him. So making love to another person actually made oneself more valuable. Hence, the more one had sex, the more one valuable one became. Tony tried to think about these issues seriously, as though he were studying a flaw in society's accepted doctrine, but he became aroused and thought about sex.

The day passed slowly. Tony felt like he was baking in his airless car. After an eternity, midnight struck, the lights in the store went off, and the manager locked the door. Starving, sleepy, and sexually aroused, Tony started his car and drove home for a cold shower and a little sleep. He wanted to make the best of the few hours he had before the store re-opened. No way was he not going to be there when the freak, and his $10,000, showed up.

CHAPTER 18

❀

Billy sat beside Melissa while he cleaned his sword and explained its history. The weapon always symbolized truth to him. It was for vanquishing evil foes and slaying mighty dragons, setting straight the wrongs done to the weak or defenseless, and protecting virtue and honor.

"At least that's the way I like to think of it. The samurai used to believe that their sword contained their soul. It was their most prized possession."

"Do you practice with it?"

"Oh, yeah. All the time. I've studied it most of my life. It's like moving meditation. I started as a kid, when I was around five. Roy thought it would help my self-esteem. I've practiced it ever since."

"You must really enjoy it."

"Yeah, I do, but it's more than that. I think it also gives me focus. I've always identified with the warrior-poet, the symbol of strength and intelligence. You know, the military is often society's most reviled sect, yet because of them, the nation exists. It's a Catch-22."

"I guess I never thought of it that way," Melissa said. "Do you write poetry?"

"A little."

"Read me some of it."

Billy panicked. "I will one day, I promise, but not right now. Nobody's ever read any of it. It's just kind of embarrassing."

"Okay." Melissa smiled, and Billy relaxed. "A warrior-poet…I like that."

"I think I relate most to their isolation within civilization. I mean, they protect our nation's freedom, and some people use that freedom to criticize their existence."

"You've put a lot of thought into this."

"It's about all I have to do with so much time alone."

"Why do spend so much time alone?"

"Well, let's just say I'm not the most popular boy in Sunday school."

"Why? You seem pretty great to me."

Billy didn't answer right away. "It's a long story," he said finally.

"So tell me about it. We have plenty of time. We don't seem to be going anywhere."

Billy took in a deep breath and exhaled sharply. Then he closed his eyes. "My earliest memory is of the orphanage where I grew up. I was always the target of everybody's jokes. I guess it gave me a bad attitude early on. I just didn't understand why I had to be different, so I got angry a lot."

"Different?"

"My face," Billy whispered.

Melissa slowly reached up and touched his face. Billy winced but did not stop her. She explored his face with her fingertips. She grimaced, a frown playing on her lips. He could only guess what was going through her mind. When she finished, she slid her hands down to his chest and laid her head on his shoulder.

"Go on," she said, as if nothing had happened.

"Well, I was always fighting. Once, in high school, a group of guys played a joke on me. They thought it was sooo funny. It was really bad. I almost beat one of the guys to death. It took all of the strings

Roy could pull to keep me from going to jail. I got five years probation instead."

"That seems so out of character! You're so gentle."

"Yeah, well a lot of people would disagree with you about that."

"And a lot of people don't know you, either."

"You think you know me?"

"Galahad," Melissa said with a shy smile.

"More like Don Quixote," Billy returned.

They both laughed.

Her eyes softened. "Maybe. After all, Quixote was a brave and noble man. He was just misunderstood."

"What about you? You haven't told me much, except that your husband is trying to kill you." He set the sword aside and wrapped his arm around her. She snuggled in closer, as if it were where she belonged.

"I married Stephen exactly six months from the day I graduated college. He spent most of his spare time with me my last year, escorting me to and from class, taking me to lunch every day." She sighed and shifted a little. Billy gently lifted a strand of hair off her cheek. "He convinced me he had this burning, undying love for me. I'd dated other boys, but mostly they just wanted to take advantage of the rich blind girl. You know what I mean. I don't know if I ever really loved Stephen, but he was so kind, and so considerate. A gentleman, always a gentleman. He wouldn't think of touching me without my permission. He made me feel…safe."

Melissa stopped talking. The memories of her foolishness seemed to waft around her head. Billy just held her and waited. Finally, she gave a little sigh and began again. "Anyway, to make a long story short, we decided to get married. My father was absolutely livid. He said Stephen was only after his money. I was so sure he was wrong! We ran away together and daddy hired a detective to find us and tell us he would consent if I came home. But when we got there, he made Stephen sign a premarital contract. He'd lose everything if we split up for any reason. Stephen wasn't happy about it and wanted me to talk daddy out of it, but daddy said he'd be forced to write me out of his will if I married Stephen without him signing. I was so…stupid," she said softly. "I didn't see. Anyway," she went with an air of resignation, "he finally signed. And he's hated me since."

"How long have you been married?"

"Almost four years."

"What about your father?"

"He died two years ago. God, I miss him! Stephen's been in control of everything since, including me. Especially me. The first thing he did was fire all the people who looked after me. He locks me in the house, he's beaten me, he…he…." She took a breath. "I don't know what to do or whom to trust. Stephen's got control of the money, for now. I've overheard his phone calls sometimes; he's got a lot of other people and power behind him now. I am afraid to even call my lawyer. You know, in Louisiana, you can do whatever you want if you shake the right hands."

"He beat you?" Billy asked, not wanting to even think about what she couldn't bring herself to say. "Why would he do that?"

"Because I tried to run away," she said. "I just couldn't stand being trapped like that." A troubled look crossed her face. "If he finds me this time, he'll kill me."

"But you said if anything happens to you, he loses everything. He wouldn't kill you. Besides," Billy said, his voice taking on an edge that came from deep inside his soul, "he'll never find you here. And even if he does, he'll have to get through me to get to you. And he won't. Believe me. I would never let him touch you."

Melissa nestled against his warm strength. "You know," she said, "when I was a child, I used to think Prince Charming would come and sweep me off my feet and we would ride off into the sunset and live happily ever after. Then I grew up and found myself married to Stephen, and realized what a foolish child I'd been. Do you know what I mean?"

"I never believed in fairy tales."

"I did." She paused. "And then for a long time I didn't." Melissa traced her finger lightly across his chest. "But now I do again."

Billy's skin prickled with pleasure at her touch. He licked his dry lips and swallowed, unable to trust his voice to speak. After a moment, Melissa went on. "You know, people forget you're still a person just because you're blind. I mean, I've been blind all my life, but that doesn't mean I don't still have hopes and dreams. Being blind doesn't change that. If anything, it makes me stronger."

Billy nodded, to himself. "I know," he said softly.

They held each other for a few more minutes. At length, Melissa stirred once more. "Okay, your turn again."

Billy grimaced. "There's nothing about me really worth talking about."

"Oh, come on, sure there is. You're the bravest, most giving person I've ever known," she whispered softly. She moved her head to rub her cheek against his shoulder.

"Bravery and stupidity are not far removed," he said.

"I think they are."

Billy laid his cheek on top of her head and inhaled deeply, savoring the sweet smell of her hair. She neither moved nor objected. He opened his mouth to speak, but no sound came out. His voice was strangled by the wild pounding in his chest and the rhythmic quivering of his insides. His heart screamed at him to sweep her into a passionate kiss, but his mind told him not to be stupid. She was soft and warm in his arms, and she clearly needed and wanted his protection—for the rest, he was undoubtedly misreading her intentions.

"The samurai lived with a constant readiness to die," he said in a tense voice. "Once the fear of death is conquered, there is nothing left to fear."

Melissa considered that. "Are you ready to die?"

"For the right cause."

"What's the right cause?"

Billy swallowed hard. "I don't think you know until you're faced with it."

"Tell me more. Don't tell me about the samurai. Tell me about you."

Slowly, Billy disentangled from Melissa. He leaned forward, propped his elbows on his knees and put his forehead into his hands. He didn't want to talk about what she wanted to hear. Even after all these years, he still couldn't think about it without his guts turning to jelly. Finally, he took a deep breath and exhaled sharply.

"When I was born," he began, "my father set me on fire and crushed my face with the heel of his boot—at least I imagine it was my father. Roy found me freezing in a trash can when I was only a few hours old." He took another deep breath. "My life has been pretty much the same since then," he finished.

"God! How awful!"

"You get used to it."

"I guess it's a lot like being blind."

He shook his head. "No. No, it's just the opposite."

Melissa groped the air, found him, and leaned herself against his strong, warm back. Her heart began to flutter as she felt his beating through his backbone. The blood rushed to her face. She pulled at him slightly, and he leaned back so she could face him. She reached up and tugged gently at his head, pulling his face next to hers, his rough, hot cheek against the tender flesh of her face. Neither spoke for a long time. Their lips hovered over each other for a moment. Then they met, lightly, briefly.

"I think…," she began, but Billy cut her off with a full, passionate kiss that made her moan. She fell against his chest.

Billy broke the kiss to suck a deep tremulous breath, gasping for air as though he might faint. He stroked her hair with both hands, stifled a cry, and kissed her again. Then he dropped back and pulled Melissa over him. Her hair hung down over his face and chest as she covered his face with kisses, soft, starved kisses of passion and longing and need. He ran his hands down her sides and the kisses got harder and more desperate. They clung to each other and rolled, until she was on her back, reaching up to pull him to her, her mouth open and searching, her body trembling with excitement and desire.

"Billy," she whispered urgently.

He buried his face in the nape of her neck, kissing and breathing in the intoxicating scent of her skin.

He pulled back for a moment to gaze down upon this angel, this wisp of a girl who lay trembling beneath him.

He moaned and covered her mouth with his and kissed her over and over and over until he could no longer hold back the tears. Tenderly now, he moved from her lips to her chin and neck, slid his hands around her back and squeezed her tightly as he pressed his hips toward her. Suddenly, everything changed. He stopped.

"What's wrong?"

"Billy, I'm scared." She took in a deep breath as tears formed in her eyes. "I've had such a bad experience. I'm afraid, Billy. I'm so sorry."

"No. No. No. Don't be sorry." Billy's heart broke under the weight of rejection. He knew he had overstepped his bounds.

"I'm sorry. I'm just not ready."

"That's okay. That's okay. I just thought…don't be sorry, please don't be sorry…I didn't mean to hurt you…I didn't mean to hurt you…please don't be sorry." The tears fell down his face in a steady stream, and his voice quivered under the intense emotion, and shame he felt.

"I think I'm falling in love with you, Billy."

He gasped so loud it startled her. He jumped to his knees. "You what?"

"I think I love you Billy. It's just that…he raped me, and beat me…and, Billy please don't pull away from me," her tears now flowing steadily. "I need you to hold me."

He fell on top of her and held her in his arms, as both started sobbing, in a moment of honest and intense emotional need.

They lay in each other's arms sharing each other's pain, and mending each other's wounds, each becoming one with the other, inseparable, and undeniable.

CHAPTER 19

※

Roy leaned both elbows on the driver's door of the squad car and peered inside at Donny Hebert and Clyde Robicheaux, two of the six officers G-man had recommended for surveillance of Billy and his guest. The six had all volunteered to moonlight, without pay, in three eight-hour shifts. That's the way it worked in southern Louisiana: you stuck together, helped your own. If one day later you were in trouble yourself and needed help, it would come without question, and without charge.

Of the two young officers, Clyde spoke with the strongest Cajun accent, though both were born and raised in the swampland. Donny had left for a while to study criminal justice at a university in Memphis, and the Yankees had influenced his fine Cajun dialect.

"How are you boys doing?" asked Roy.

"Doing fine. What about yourself?" Donny answered.

"Oh, I could complain, but nobody wants to hear it." Roy smiled. "Hey guys, I really appreciate the help here."

Clyde leaned forward. "Not a problem. If I was home I would have to visit with mother-in-law anyway, yah."

All three laughed.

"Are you boys hungry? Anything I can get you?"

"I'm starving." Donny returned quickly.

"What would you like?"

"What I would like is a huge bucket of crawfish, but I'll take whatever I can get."

"You?" Roy asked Clyde.

"No matter. Whatever you get is fine."

"Be right back." Neither Donny nor Clyde had offered any money. Roy hadn't expected them to.

Stephen paced nervously back and forth in front of his desk. "Five days," he spat. "Almost a week and we haven't heard a thing."

"Calm down," returned Anderson. "David said we have everything covered. They'll turn up. If they're in the city, we'll find them."

"Yeah, well, what if they're not still in the city?"

Anderson sat back in the chair and absently scratched his chin. After a moment, he shrugged mentally and changed the subject. "David said maybe you should try to have her declared incompetent once we get her back. You could get her confined to a nursing home or institution to start, then we arrange to make it permanent. That way, she's under guard 24-hours a day, and you have access to all the money until she dies of natural causes—or an accident."

"Won't work." Stephen shook his head. "The only way to make sure things don't go wrong is to tie up the loose ends, and she is a loose end." Stephen fingered the bandage on the side of his face. "Besides, I really want that ugly freak!"

Anderson simply nodded. He'd seen Stephen in these kinds of fits all his life. By now, he knew well enough that no matter what he said, it would be wrong, so he just shifted in his seat and stared out the window.

"I'm getting very impatient!" Stephen scowled.

Anderson sighed under his breath. "Just calm down. She'll turn up," he offered aloud, but his mind was on the conversation he'd had earlier with David. It had been a stroke of genius on his part to find such an accommodating layer. David had everything under control, even if Stephen did not—at least as far as Anderson was concerned.

Stephen was still pacing. Morons surround me, he fumed to himself. What if somebody's already found her and she made a better deal with them herself? "Not good," he growled, his words following his inner thoughts. "Anything could go wrong here. Anything. She's not stupid! This is extremely not good."

"For God's sakes, stop worrying! I talked to David this morning. He said everything would be fine."

"Would you shut up about David, already? I don't give a flying flip about what David said!"

Anderson narrowed his eyes and looked away. Stephen never noticed.

"You get these people on the ball, you understand? Do something right for once in your pathetic life! I want her back here yesterday, and I expect you to take care of it! Understand?"

Anderson just nodded. His mind was running in a million directions, too full of his own plans and schemes to give much heed to his brother's latest verbal assault.

Roy handed two greasy brown-paper bags through the driver's window to Donny, who, in turn, handed one to Clyde. The smell of hot crawfish filled the car.

"How about crawfish po-boys?" Roy offered. "All they had were sandwiches. These were the best compromise I could come up with between boiled crawfish and ham-and-cheese."

"Great," Clyde said, his mouth already full. "Let the good times roll."

Roy smiled. "You boys enjoy your supper, now. I'm going in to check on our package."

Roy crossed the street and hopped up the rickety steps to the Hot Spot. The motorcycles lining the curb indicated that most of the regulars had already arrived. He stopped inside for a few minutes to allow his eyes to adjust to the dim light and smoke in the room. All the barstools were filled and a game was going at the pool table, but the tables were still relatively empty because the girls had not yet started dancing.

Billy's door opened and Melissa stepped out. Roy inhaled sharply. What's the matter with that girl? he thought. Walking right out in front of everybody—I told her to stay hidden. He watched her feel her way to the bar and lean forward.

"May I have a glass of water, please?"

The bikers in the bar sat transfixed on the beautiful woman who looked completely out of place among them. One of the men, a skinny hippie type, walked around behind Melissa and worked his hands only inches from her behind as though squeezing her butt. He closed his eyes and puckered his lips as if he could hardly control himself. The other bikers at the bar laughed, which spurred on the skinny man on. He started moving his hips back and forth as though having sex with her. Everyone laughed.

Suddenly Billy appeared, and kicked the skinny man squarely in the ass. The bikers at the bar roared hilariously. Some fell off their seats, and others held their midsections with their hands while their bellies shook and their faces reddened from the intense uncontrollable laughter.

"Hey man!" the skinny man exclaimed, grabbing at his backside with both hands and sounding truly surprised. "Why'd you kick me?"

"Sit your ass down over there and learn to show some respect."

"Hey, I was just having fun."

The middle-aged hippie pouted as he walked back to his seat. Billy moved behind Melissa, put his arms around her waist and hugged her tightly. He leaned down to kiss her on the neck. The move was greeted with whistles and catcalls.

"All right, Billy Boy!" someone shouted.

Roy had watched the whole scene silently, but cringed when he saw Billy kiss the young heiress and almost cried out when she tilted her head to the side to return the kiss. Oh, man. *This is only going to complicate an already bad situation…*

James set a glass of water on the bar in front of Melissa. "Hey, break it up you two," he joked. "You'll give the place a bad reputation."

"I didn't know it could get any worse," Billy shot back.

"Funny. That's very funny. Maybe you should get on the stage and entertain us."

Billy's face glowed as he led Melissa back to his room. Unnoticed, Roy eased out the front door. He stood thinking for a moment, then sighed deeply and shook his head. Everything seemed all right now, but his instinct told him it wasn't going to stay that way. He waved absently at the two officers as he walked down the street toward his car, still thinking hard.

CHAPTER 20

Billy emerged from the gloomy bar and blinked against New Orlean's hazy morning sunshine. He quickly spotted Buster Rabalais and Ron Johnston pretending to not be policemen in an unmarked car across the street.

"Morning," Buster said as Billy came up and leaned into the window.

"Morning," he returned. "You guys been here long?"

"Just a few minutes."

"I'm just going down to the store for some stuff. You guys need anything?"

"No," Buster said, "but I think you should let us go and pick up whatever you need. You should stay put."

"I'd rather have you guys watching her," Billy said, motioning with his head toward the Hot Spot.

Ron opened the door popped his head over the top of the car from the passenger's side. "Well, I'd better go with you, just to be safe."

Billy shrugged. "There's no need, but if you wanna stretch your legs, you're welcome to tag along."

"What are you so happy about?" Ron teased. "You act like you got lucky."

"Lucky doesn't even come close."

Buster gaped out the window. "Well, I'll be—Billy's in love."

Three weeks ago, Billy would have lost his temper, and maybe even put his fist through the guy's face. Now, he just blushed behind a sheepish grin.

"Well, congrats, Bud." Ron came around the car and reached out to shake Billy's hand. "It's nice to see you smile."

"It's been a long time since I've had anything to smile about."

Ron slapped Billy on the shoulder, and started telling him a story about one of his old girlfriends as they walked together toward the store.

Tony Masca dropped another cigarette out the driver's window and scanned the empty parking lot with half-closed eyes. His back was propped up against the door, one foot braced on the dash, the other splayed across the seat. The song coming out of car radio had already been played twice already, and it was still relatively early. Although bored out of his mind, he had faithfully stood his post for six days now. Patience usually paid off in these situations, but he was just about at the point where he was going to try and think another course of action. For all he knew, the fugitives could have already left the city while he sat there waiting and wasting time.

He pushed in the lighter on the dash and fished another cigarette from the flip-top box in his shirt pocket. The bright red coils touched the tobacco, and he took a long first drag. It tasted awful, the result of smoking too much and eating too little for too many days in a row. He pulled at his sweat-soaked shirt, already drenched from the unrelenting heat, heightened to torturous levels inside his airless vehicle. He'd have to go in the air-conditioned store for something to drink before long, but the thought of eating in his heat made him feel green. He took another unsatisfying drag from the soggy butt, tilting his head back on the headrest to exhale the smoke upward and watch it cause ripples in the cloth hanging from the car's roof. Another drag, more smoke rings spreading into bigger and bigger circles as they moved around the material above. Finally, he threw the half-smoked cigarette out the window, shifted in his seat, and reached for the door handle. He had just placed one foot on the concrete when he froze.

"Well, its about time," he mumbled to himself. There was the freak with some other guy, rounding the corner and going into the store. As soon as he saw them disappear inside, he jumped from the car and moved quickly to a position a block or so away in the direction from which they had come. He found a shady spot and waited.

At length, the two walked back past him. Tony stretched, scratched at his chin, and sauntered along behind them, far enough behind that no one would notice. Several blocks and numerous turns later, the freak went into a bar, and the other guy walked over to a car across the street and got in on the passenger's side. Cop, Tony recognized. Thought so. Pretty obvious.

Tony continued past the bar, made a mental note of the address and nodded to the two men pretending not to watch him. He went around the corner at the end of the block and circled back to his own car.

After driving back to his apartment/office, Tony opened a cold beer, took a few swallows, propped his feet on the coffee table and finally allowed himself to breathe a sigh of relief. He'd found the girl—the ten thou was his. All he had to do was pass on the information.

Money, after all, made the world go around; finally, he could give the globe a couple of spins. Money got things done. One thing he did not quite understand was why the green paper was valuable. He knew gold had been used years ago. Gold is indestructible; the flimsy paper that took its place is easily destroyed. How long had people used gold as a means of barter? The world's oldest profession had used gold. What would one of them think of his worthless paper money? Tony tried to think about these questions seriously, as though he were studying a flaw in society's accepted doctrine, but he became aroused and thought about sex.

CHAPTER 21

❀

Stephen's face gleamed as he clicked off the phone. He clapped his hands, shook both fists over his head and shouted, "YES!" Then he hit the speed-dial button to Anderson's cellular phone.

"Hello?"

"We've got them," Stephen half shouted.

"Great. Where are they?"

"At some bar in the French Quarter. The ah...," Stephen glanced down at his note pad. "Hot Spot. Get over here now, understand? I'm going to make a few calls and get some people down there today!"

Stephen clicked off the phone and clapped his hands together again before grabbing his address book and looking up Jon Martin. Jon had done several jobs in the past, always with good results. Stephen liked that he never met with anyone except Jon, and that none of Jon's men ever even knew whom they were working for. Anonymity was essential in many of Stephen's dealings, and Jon had always made him feel secure. Of course, when Jon stopped making him feel secure, he'd no longer be of any use at all.

Jon answered the phone himself, and in just a few short minutes, the plan was in progress. He'd put together a good team, retrieve the girl, and deliver her to the Pruit mansion that night. Stephen agreed to pay him $50,000 upon delivery—not bad for a few hours' work.

Jon Martin calmly picked up the phone and started making phone calls. Fifty thousand—not bad, but not the best either. Two of his regular men were unavailable, but one suggested a couple of guys he had worked with on some earlier jobs: Eric Zimmer and George Hall. Jon normally didn't hire men sight unseen, but with such short notice, any manpower would have to do. He told everyone to meet at his place at 3:00 p.m. to go over the plan.

At 8:45 p.m., two shiny black Mercedes glided to the curb in front of the Hot Spot, just a few feet from a long row of motorcycles. George Hall, wearing a suit that made him look more like a businessman than a thug, nodded at the two men sitting in the unmarked police car across the street, then strolled over to them.

"He could be the poster for the Most Beautiful Man in America contest," Jon smirked.

George extended a manicured hand into the car to shake hands with the driver.

"George Hall," he said. "I am sorry to trouble you, officer, but we were looking for the Landmark Hotel. We were supposed to be there at 8:00 for a banquet, but we can't seem to find the darn place." He smiled sheepishly.

"Man, you're way off. That's back down along the interstate. Back about ten miles."

"Can you give me directions? Better yet…." George motioned for Eric to join him. "Eric's our driver. It'd be better if you told him."

Eric moved around to the passenger side of the car and leaned in at the window. George slipped a Breatta 9mm out of his pocket, complete with silencer. While the officers talked to Eric, George raised the pistol over the edge of the car door. He eased the gun into position and with a whisper sent a lead pellet through the head of the officer. A mesh of brain, bone, and blood splattered across the right side of the car. The other cop quickly turned his head to see what had happened but, before he even had time to see his dead partner, a bullet went through his forehead, out the base of his skull, and embedded in the car door.

The two officers lay dead less than two minutes from the time the two Mercedes had parked.

The rest of the men were waiting for them at the front of the Hot Spot. Making their entrance together lent the performance a more intimidating quality, and kept them positioned to watch each other's backs. They walked up the stairs as a group, opened the door, and stepped inside the bar.

Jon immediately spotted Billy standing by the jukebox. Billy folded his across his chest and trained his eyes on the newcomers. Jon and his men made their way toward him, trying to avoid the groups of people sitting, but bumping into more than a few as they wove through the dim room. Passing the pool table, Jon knocked into a biker about to take a shot. The biker missed.

"Hey, watch where you're going, fancy pants!" he growled.

"Pardon me," he apologized. He did not want to get off-track. The job came first.

"Pardon this!" the biker said, grabbing his groin. A number of men in the area laughed.

"You'd better watch that, man. Pretty boy there may like that!"

"Yeah, he sure is awful pretty for a man."

"Hell, he's better lookin' than your girlfriend!"

The biker who had been bumped turned back to the table. "I get that shot over," he said, returning the balls to the where they had sat before the interruption. No one objected.

The group of suits spread out in front of Billy, who stood narrow-eyed and unflinching. Jon stood moved in close enough to be heard. James flipped the power switch for the jukebox, and the room was suddenly painfully silent. Everyone watched.

"Where's the girl?"

Billy neither moved nor spoke.

"Where's the girl?" Jon asked louder.

Billy remained silent.

Jon made his face mean and his voice nasty. "I said," he began, reaching up to grab Billy, "where's the…."

Billy caught Jon's hand in mid-air, and in one smooth motion, swung it to the side and slammed Jon's head into the jukebox. Snickers scattered across the room. Jon looked up from the floor, astonished. A smudge of bright-red blood was dripping from one cheekbone. He grabbed for his pistol, but before he level it into place, one of the pool players struck his arm with a cue stick. The gun flew out of Jon's hand.

"Let's keep it fair, now," the biker admonished. He scooped up the pistol, hefted it for comfort, and put it in his pocket.

Jon grunted and all his men started to rush Billy at once. Eric reached for his gun, but before he could get it clear of his coat, the biker shoved Jon's pistol to his head. They stopped at the click of the hammer being pulled back. Instinctively turning toward the sound *en masse*, they found the biker holding Jon's cocked pistol to Eric's temple. Jon was still on the floor, a booted foot now resting heavily on his neck.

"No, no, now," the biker said. "Let's keep it fair, I said. One on one."

The other pool players and the rest of their bar buddies quickly moved in and disarmed the intruders, snatching weapons away from them as if they were taking toys from a bunch of toddlers.

"Hey, check this out."

"Man, lookie what I got."

"Hey, lemme see that. Wanna trade?"

The regulars bartered and traded weapons while the intruders looked on, and then at each other. The man with his foot on Jon's neck allowed him to get up and moved him next to the other suits. One of the bikers came up from behind and pushed one of the intruders toward Billy. The rest of the crowd encircled the combatants.

"You want him? Go get him." An undercurrent of excitement rolled through the crowd.

"All we want is the girl," Jon said, half to Billy, half to the watchers.

"You can't have her," Billy answered flatly.

"Fight him!" one of the bikers called. "If you beat him, hell, we'll give you the girl." The regulars laughed. Someone pushed the man another step toward Billy. Almost without effort, Billy broke a few major bones and sent him groaning to the floor. The crowd cheered. Money changed hands.

The bikers pulled the battered guy to the side and pushed in another. Billy didn't bother to wait for the attack. He smashed the man on the side of the head with a hammer-fist strike. The man staggered, shook his head, swayed again, and slumped to the floor, blood dripping from his left ear.

The bikers booed. "Aw, come on, you can do better than that!" one of them sneered. They shoved a knife into the next victim's hand and tossed one to Billy.

The man staggered forward slowly, like a gladiator sent to his death for the amusement of a cheering audience of bloodthirsty Romans. He half-heartedly flicked his knife at Billy, and pulled back quickly, but when he drew his hand up, it was bleeding. He looked in wonder at the streaming blood. He hadn't even seen his opponent move.

The crowd was cheering. "Go get 'em, you twerp!"

Billy reversed his grip on the knife. The man, caught between anger and humiliation and promised pain from all comers, shook the red off his hand and lunged. Billy shuffled right, grabbed the attacker's wrist and made an almost surgical cut across the tendons. The knife fell, the injured man clenched his hand to his chest, and Billy lifted his foot to the man's groin and shoved him back into the crowd.

"These guys suck!"

"Send in two!"

"Yeah, come on, let's see some action, for chrissake! These guys ain't nothin'."

George and Eric found themselves pushed into the center of the ring. They looked sideways at each other with a shared confidence and attacked simultaneously. They dropped together, too, their heads slammed against each other several times before they'd even had a chance to show off their practiced, never-fail timing.

Billy turned to Jon, the only suit still standing. "Tell him to leave us alone," he said calmly. "Tell him, we don't want the money. Tell him, he can have the money. We don't want anything to do with him. Melissa is fine where she is."

Jon didn't answer. Billy gestured impatiently. "Nod your head if you understand what I just said," he instructed.

Jon nodded slowly. The wound on his cheek had stopped bleeding, but his hair was soaked, and his eyes dazed and glassy. He swayed from side to side as though the slightest breeze would make him fall. Billy palm gripped Jon's forehead and turned his face to look eye to eye with him. Billy shook his head in disgust and pushed him to the floor. The bikers cheered, and reached from every direction to pat Billy on the back.

A young man known only as T-Bo walked in through the front door and shouted, "Hey, listen up! There are two dead guys out here! Cops!"

In the din that followed, the bikers decided to tie up the suits in one big bundle, the to keep an eye on them. James motioned Billy to the bar.

"You know," he said, leaning across the polished wood to be heard, "you and the girl are gonna to have to leave. They know where you are now, and they're not gonna stop. Next time they won't underestimate things, either."

"Yeah, I know," Billy answered gravely.

"Listen up!" James bellowed. The commotion in the bar dwindled. "Billy here needs to disappear for a while. Him and his girl."

Billy smiled at hearing Melissa called "his girl." The bar regulars, certainly not new to "disappearing" and commanding an 'ole boy network among them unrivaled by any other, gathered around to make a plan. After careful consideration, their consensus was that Billy and Melissa needed to get out of New Orleans. The only problem was, as always, a lack of money.

"I got it," T-Bo shouted over the other voices in the crowd. Everyone knew that from that moment it was T-Bo's responsibility to get Billy and the girl out of town. No one would dare ask how, when, or where—no one else needed to know. As soon as they were gone T-Bo's job would be to disappear.

T-Bo pulled Billy to the side. "You know how to ride, don't you?" he asked, dropping the keys to his motorcycle into the young man's hand.

"How hard can it be?" Billy joked. He didn't ask why T-Bo was doing this for him, or why the bikers—most of whom he'd beaten up at one time or another—had all gotten behind him. He just went with it, savoring this unique experience of being "one of the guys," and feeling the strength that comes from being accepted.

T-Bo leaned over and whispered in Billy's ear at length then stood back. "I'll put in a call as soon as you leave," T-Bo continued aloud with a touch of pride in his voice. "They'll be expecting you." Having found a suitable hiding place, his value in the rough, loosely formed cadre had risen to hero status.

"Nobody here knows where I am going do they?"

"No."

Billy went back to his room to get Melissa, and found her huddled into one corner, trembling. As soon as she heard his voice, she ran toward it. He held her tightly while he explained that they'd have to leave for a while. "You'll have to trust me," he said, stroking her hair.

"You know I do."

"I have to get you away from here. I have to get you to a safe place. I won't let him take you back."

"Whatever you say, Billy. I'll do whatever you say. I just want to stay with you."

It took only a few minutes for Billy to gather his belongings and the few changes of clothing he'd managed to pick up for Melissa.

The majority of the crowd moved outside to examine the dead men. One of the bikers walked up to Jon and kicked him in the leg.

"On your feet," he ordered.

Jon staggered to his feet in unison with the other men tied to him in a giant bundle of flesh.

The biker shoved them toward the door with his foot. "Outside," he barked. "I ain't letting you guys out of my sight."

The group of captives moved toward the door stumbling and staggering. Once out the door the biker shoved them again and the whole group tumbled down the steps and landed in a heap on the sidewalk.

Outside, T-Bo helped Melissa onto the bike behind Billy, and fastened his helmet to her head as Billy revved the motor.

"How will I know them?" Billy asked.

"Don't worry about that," T-Bo answered, "they'll know you. You'd better go now. We've already called the cops." T-Bo nodded toward the two dead officers in the unmarked police car.

Perhaps it was because he didn't want to return empty handed. Or maybe it was because of his ability to focus under pressure, but Jon noticed something that on one else did. The license place on the bike read 'motor -1'.

Billy revved the motor a few more times and took off. The darkness soon swallowed any sign of the bike and its riders. T-Bo also disappeared into the darkness just moments before the first of half-a-dozen police cars came screeching to a halt in front of what was now the hottest spot in New Orleans.

CHAPTER 22

The coroner's men hadn't yet removed the bodies when Roy heard the news over his police scanner and made a beeline to the bar. The scene was one with which he was too familiar: six patrol cars, two ambulances, officers milling about everywhere taking fingerprints, photographs, and statements from the bar patrons who were complaining loudly about not being able to leave.

Roy made his way to James and pulled him by the elbow off to the side. "Where's Billy?"

"On his way out of town. He got out of here before this circus started."

Roy sucked air between his teeth. "I should have put her into protective custody from the beginning," he said, half irritated with himself, half relieved that she and Billy had gotten safely away. "Where?"

James shrugged. "I don't know. Ask the guy who lent them the bike."

"Which one?"

James pointed. "The black guy. Over…" James looked around the crowd. "I don't see him. Goes by T-Bo."

"Shit. Who else would know?"

James thought before he answered. "No one—you know how this works."

Roy sighed. "So what happened here?"

"Bunch of fancy-dressed thugs came to take Melissa away, Billy busted them up pretty good—then took off. When the cops showed up, they didn't even know why these guys were watching the place." James motioned toward the dead cops. "Nobody's mentioned Billy's name, yet, and I don't think they will, but the suits might. The story is just that these guys showed up, killed the cops, and tried to break up the place. You'd be amazed at how many of my upstanding, regular patrons were willing to take the credit for stopping them."

Roy gave a forced smile. "Yeah, well, best to keep it that way for now." He exhaled sharply. "Only six people from our side know about the girl. I can trust them to keep it quiet until this is settled, but these guys…." Roy nodded toward the mob of cops. "They're going to want some retribution over this. Not that I wouldn't like some myself," he said, almost to himself. After all, he had asked them to stand the post, and on their own time, too. Now their wives were widows. And the man he had long come to think of as his son was on the lam, running into who-knew-what danger. He had underplayed his hand. He would not do it again.

Roy started to walk away. "Try not to worry about him," James called.

Roy turned back. His eyes met James'. "Yeah, right. If you see this guy T-Bo call me."

"I will. I mean it. I gave Billy a couple hundred dollars." James paused for a second and exhaled. "It was all I had. But he's a big boy. He'll be fine."

Roy pursed his lips and nodded.

"Worrying is just going to make you age faster. It certainly won't help Billy."

"Yeah, well, thanks," Roy said. "Really. I'll get the money back to you as soon as I can."

James shook his head. "Forget it. I just wish I could have done more." James smiled and his eyes softened. "You should have been around him these last few days. He was a different person."

"I knew he was falling hard for the girl."

"Hard ain't even close. That boy is crazy in love and, oddly enough, I think she is, too." His smile widened even further.

Roy allowed himself a half smile, and looked around the scene. His head felt like it was bursting, his thoughts running in a dozen different directions. He scratched at his hairline and shook it off. "Call me if you see T-Bo. I can't really put out a bulletin on him. I can't afford to let anyone else know. Too many loose ends already…. besides, I don't even have a real name."

Billy drove the bike across the Lake Pontchartrain causeway at 90 mph with Melissa clinging to him from the rear. His eyes kept darting from the rearview mirror to the road ahead. He could count the number of times he'd ever been out of New Orleans on one hand, but panic had filled him with an urgency to get Melissa out of the city as fast as he could. He only wished he could be sure he was headed in the right direction. It's big motor screaming, the motorcycle pushed on into the night. After a couple of hours, Billy saw the sign for Highland Road T-Bo had told him about, and allowed himself a fleeting second of relief.

He took a right on Highland Road, another right by a water park and followed the twisting, turning road until it turned to gravel. Presently, they came upon a small group of run-down buildings.

Billy parked the bike and helped Melissa off. The smell of fish thickened the damp night air. He looked around. "Man, I hope this is the right place," he muttered under his breath.

"Where are we?" Melissa asked.

Billy put a reassuring smile in his voice. "I think we're where we're supposed to be."

The edge of some body of water, only about 60 yards from the road, gave the air a musty feel. A tiny white building off to the side had a GENERAL STORE AND BAIT SHOP sign over the front door. Another building a few yards away sat propped off the ground with cement blocks. Decrepit, unleveled, covered with beer signs and surrounded by empties, its sign read, "Alligator Hilton." A few trailers were raised high off the ground on wooden pillions.

The small community lay deathly quiet, flooded only in the bright glow of the moon. Billy had no trouble making out the surrounding area or even the expressions on his angel's face, which seemed rather strange. He rarely saw more than a few stars at a time in the city, but here, the sky practically glittered, like a million tiny diamonds on a black velvet cloth. He caught his breath in wonder, the pursuing danger momentarily forgotten.

"What is it? What's wrong?"

"Nothing." Billy took Melissa's hand and pulled her close to his side. "This must be the place," he said.

Immediately after he spoke, a little old black man hobbled around the corner of the general store footsteps scuffling along in the gravel toward them. He had apparently been hiding in the shadows behind the building watching.

He halted a few feet away and looked them over. Then he said, "This way, son," and hobbled off toward the water.

Billy guided Melissa over the rough terrain toward the old man's boat, then went back and pushed the motorcycle into the little space between the store and the Alligator Hilton. Satisfied that a casual passerby could not see it from the road, he quickly returned to her side.

"Hop in," the old man said. He sat in the rear of the boat and spat tobacco juice in the water. "Careful now," he called from the darkness.

Billy got in and told Melissa to take hold of his forearms and step high to get into the boat. She gasped several times as the small craft rocked back and forth under her feet. She stumbled on something on the bottom of the boat, but Billy kept her from falling. Her nails dug into Billy's flesh as she clamped vigorously onto his arms, but he merely clenched his teeth and said nothing. Billy finally got her seated and as comfortable as she was going to be. He sat beside her, and the old man pushed the boat away from the bank with a long paddle. After a while, the only sounds were the water lightly slapping the bottom of the craft, and the frogs, crickets, and other wildlife.

The old man paddled until they'd gotten well past a bend in the canal. Then he started a small motor mounted on the back of the boat and the little flat-bottom craft took off skipping across the top of the water, it's nose bouncing against the small waves. Billy felt like they were flying. He tightened his arm around Melissa to reassure her and she clung back. In reality, the little motor only could only push the boat at a top speed of 12 to 15 mph under the best wind and water conditions. Tonight, the turbulent water was making the small engine to work twice as hard to gain half the normal speed.

The boat turned slightly and headed into a black void that lined the bank under an overhang of ghostly trees that looked like monstrous guards standing watch, ready to devour unwelcome intruders. Big branches reached out like arms with long, mossy fingers that hung down and threatened to snatch up the unsuspecting. As the boat slipped into the utter darkness, Billy felt vulnerable, weak, and completely blind. A shiver ran down his spine. He leaned over and kissed his brave little angel's cheek. After a few seconds his eyes began to adjust, and shapes and shadows began to take form. Shortly, his body swayed forward as the boat docked itself on a soft, muddy bank. The old man hobbled past, hopped onto the embankment, grabbed a rope tied to the front of the boat and pulled the craft halfway up on the land.

"Ya'll can get out now," he said. He shuffled back a few steps to give them room.

Billy helped Melissa out of the boat. She took a few steps, then bounced up and down.

"Ah, land. That feels better," she said with a sigh.

"You'll get used to the water after awhile, Miss," the old man said from somewhere in the blackness. "Just takes a little time, that's all."

Billy strained his eyes in the direction of the voice, but could barely make out a dark shadow in the blackness under the trees. "I really appreciate the help," he said.

"Oh, don't worry none about that."

"Yes, thank you, very much," Melissa seconded.

"Well, ya'll come on in and let's get you bedded down for the night. We'll chat more in the morning."

Come in? Billy thought. To what? He couldn't see anything in the darkness, no light, no house, no "inside" to head toward.

"Walter?" The voice was frail, female, and close by, but higher up.

"Sure, yeah that's me."

"You got them kids?"

"Yes, ma'am, they here with me. We coming on up." The old man shuffled a few steps ahead. Billy hooked Melissa's hand to his arm and followed.

"That's my wife, Mary." Something in the simple way the old man said his wife's name suggested an inseparable bond between them, and a homespun contentment with life that made Billy feel like he and Melissa were, indeed, in a good place. He led Melissa behind the old man for a few more yards, until they came out from under the edge of the trees. Here, the moonlight shone down brighter, and Billy could see the shadowy outline of a small house.

"Watch your step."

Billy helped Melissa slowly climb the front steps to the porch.

"Ya'll come on in," said the female voice. A screen door moved back and forth on rusty, squeaky hinges.

"I can't see anything," Billy said, hoping he would inspire them to turn on a light.

"Oh, I'm so sorry. We been here so long we hardly use lights at night. Just know where everything is."

A match was struck, the small yellow light illuminating the glowing face of an elderly black woman whose big, toothless smile seemed to go from ear to ear. Her almost completely gray hair was pulled back in a bun, and her eyes glowed with a warm, motherly kindness. Her work-worn hands trembled slightly as she lit an oil lantern. She reset the globe and put the lantern on a small wooden table, lighting up the place with a dim, dancing light that cast eerie shadows on the walls from everything in its path.

Billy managed to lead Melissa through the front door into the small, modestly furnished, two-room cabin. The kitchen doubled as a living room; the bedroom was apparently through the only other door. There didn't seem to be any room for a bathroom. Mary had spread out a blanket on the living-room floor and laid a couple of homemade pillows on one end.

Mary folded her hands on her chest, placed them under her chin, and again showed her big, warm, toothless smile. "Welcome," she said, with unmistakable enthusiasm. "Make yourselves at home." She motioned toward the blanket on the floor. "I made you a bed."

"Thank you," Billy said. He eased Melissa down onto the blanket.

"Are you hungry? Can I fix you something to eat?"

"No, thank you," Melissa answered, still clinging to Billy's arm.

"Come on, now, let these kids get some rest," Walter urged. "We can chat in the morning."

The elderly couple walked into the other room and softly closed the door behind them.

Billy helped Melissa get settled on the blanket, fixed a pillow under her head, and fetched the lamp to the side of the bed. By the time he'd returned, she was already fast asleep. Billy gazed at her face in the fiery light for a moment, then kissed her on the cheek, blew out the lamp, and cuddled up behind her. Nuzzling his nose into her hair, he drifted off to sleep with a contented smile.

CHAPTER 23

❈

Singing birds and the smell of fresh coffee woke Billy the next morning. He opened his eyes and looked around. For a moment, he was confused, unable to comprehend his surroundings. Then a flash of panic hit as he came to himself and realized that Melissa was not beside him. He sat up with a start.

"Oh, I'm sorry," Mary smiled. "I didn't mean to wake you." She stood in front of an old wood stove with an apron tied neatly around her waist. The cabin felt hot, the smell of fresh burning wood permeating the air.

"No, that's okay, you didn't." Billy rubbed his eyes with his right thumb and index finger. "Where's Melissa—the girl who was with me?"

"She's out on the porch drinking a little coffee with Walter. Would you like a little coffee?" Mary asked, her smile ever-present, her hospitality beaming.

"Yes ma'am. Please."

Mary poured a cup and put the pot back on the wood stove. "There's some sugar and a little cream over here," she said, pointing to a row of containers. "The blue one is sugar, the white one cream. The biscuits will be ready in a bit."

Billy stretched leisurely before folding the blanket and placing it neatly to the side with the pillows on top. He waited while Mary put the last few biscuits on the baking sheet, then followed her out the front door.

"Good morning, son," Walter called from his rocking chair. He had a cup of coffee in one hand and a bible open on his lap.

"About time, sleepy head," Melissa smiled. Her hand searched the air. Billy quickly stepped to her side and took it in his.

The morning sun peeked through the tops of the trees to cast a fiery red reflection that moved slowly on top of the water. The boat they'd come in sat half ashore just a few yards to the front of the little cabin. It had seemed a lot farther away in the dark.

"Good morning," Billy said in his deep morning voice. He carefully slid down beside Melissa and leaned back against the wall.

"Sorry you have to sit on the floor," Walter apologized. "I offered the young lady my chair, but she wouldn't take it." Mary had settled into the second rocking chair, beside Walter.

"This is fine," Billy returned. "It sure is nice out here."

"It's so peaceful," Melissa tilted her head so the warmth of the morning sun could rest on her face.

"Sure is," Walter agreed, sipping from his cup. "It sure is."

Moss hung from the cypress trees and cast elongated shadowy reflections on the water and mud bank. The cabin sat on polls at least ten feet off the ground to protect it from rising water. Billy wondered how many mornings this old couple had sat out there side-by-side watching the sunrise. He sipped the strong, black coffee and inhaled deeply.

"Thaddeus called up to the grocery store last night to say you'd be coming. Good thing Mrs. Brown just happened to be walking by. The store had already closed, but she ran in to get the phone, anyway and then came on out here to tell us."

"Thaddeus?" Billy questioned.

"You city boys call him T-Bo, I never did like that. Nothing wrong with Thaddeus, it's a good name."

"You don't have a phone?" Melissa asked.

"Nah." Walter laughed. "Phone company hadn't got out this far yet."

"We waiting for them, though." Mary put her hand over her mouth to hide her toothless grin.

"I hope we aren't too much trouble," Billy started.

"No, no, no," Walter cut in. "Old Mary here is just happy to have some company." Mary slapped him on the leg with one hand and covered her smile with the other. Walter leaned back and laughed out loud. Mary waved her hand in the air several times, and got up to go inside and check on the food. Walter leaned closer to Billy. "I embarrassed the girl," he said, as if talking about a teenager whose father was showing her naked baby pictures to her first boyfriend. His wrinkled, leathery skin sat heavily on his facial bones surrounding his sunken, bloodshot eyes. His salt and pepper hair had receded to the middle of his head, and when he smiled, only three yellow teeth showed. But his voice was kind and soothing.

"I hope everybody like eggs," Mary called from the house. "Breakfast is just about ready."

Billy cradled his cup in his hands, Melissa laid her head on his shoulder, and Walter rocked back and forth, back and forth, enjoying the company and the sunrise. Shortly, he began to speak with a strange mixture of sadness and pride. "She was only fourteen when I married her. She was with child just a few months after that. One day I'd gone hunting, and while I was gone, Mary gave birth to our first child. The nearest neighbor lived 15 miles away. If I'd a'known, I never would've left, but it was winter, and we were hungry. The canned crops from summer were running low.

"When the pain started, she walked the floor and prayed. Poor thing was scared to death." His voice cracked and wavered. "She'd never been around a birthing, nor many pregnant women, neither. When the pain got too much, she just lay down on the bed. She'd put a pan of water close by, and she'd a wet cloth to wipe the sweat off her face. As cold as it was outside, she was covered with sweat.

"Fourteen hours. She birthed for fourteen hours before she had the boy. She was so tired, she must've passed out. By the time I got home, the boy was dead. Mary almost died, too. She was in bed more than a week. I never left her alone again."

Walter exhaled loudly. He stared out over the trees as he rocked back and forth, back and forth. He pressed the palm of his grizzled hand into first one cheek, then the other.

"Poor Mary," Melissa whispered.

"Anyway," Walter started again, "you take care of that girl, boy. You take care of each other, and you won't have any devils when you're old like me."

"Breakfast's ready," Mary called.

Walter snapped back into the present and his face brightened. He picked up the momentum with his rocker, then rocked forward hard, threw his feet under him, and stood. "You'd better come on, this old girl can cook now!"

Billy helped Melissa to her feet and guided her into the house to her place at the small table.

"This smells wonderful," she said, feeling the table to locate utensils.

"Thank you," Mary smiled.

"It looks good, too," added Billy.

"And you can bet it is good, too, and if you don't stop your yapping, I'm going to eat it all up," Walter laughed as he piled his plate with scrambled eggs and bacon.

Billy fixed his and Melissa's plates with a little of everything: scrambled eggs, bacon, grits, biscuits, and fresh milk. He didn't want to appear rude or unappreciative. Besides, the heavenly aroma could have made him hungry on a full stomach.

After the meal, everyone went back out on the porch to rest while their food digested. The sun had moved fully over the trees and no longer cast eerie shadows. A couple of dogs Billy hadn't noticed earlier lay in the front yard.

"I've gotta go check the trout lines in a bit. You like to go?" Walter asked Billy.

"Yes, sir. I'll be happy to do whatever you need to me do."

"I don't need you to do it, I just thought maybe you'd like to go, that's all," Walter said. "Mary usually goes with me, but maybe we should let these two look after each other and do some girl talking. I suppose you can stay and do some girl talking, too, if you like." Walter burst out laughing. Billy had no idea what was so funny, but watching the little old man made him giggle, too. Mary covered her mouth with her apron and laughed quietly to herself.

"What's so funny?" Melissa asked, unable to keep from smiling herself.

"I don't know," Billy chuckled. "I guess entertainment is scarce out here."

Presently, Walter took Billy to the boat and paddled away. Once he'd gone far enough from the bank, he started the motor and the boat went flying. The old man expertly guided the boat through the swamp at top speed, never once even grazing a tree or cypress stump. They didn't seem to be traveling nearly as fast as the night before. A few minutes later, Walter shut off the motor and paddled up to an old plastic milk jug floating in the water. He lifted the jug. A string about 25 yards long was tied to the bottom with shorter strings, each about four inches long and hung with a fishing hook, attached at 18-inch intervals.

Walter lifted the string, hook by empty hook, until he came upon a half-eaten catfish.

"Those blame snapping turtles!" Walter exclaimed, tossing the fish away. It plopped into the water. He continued to pull the line until he found three fish still alive and intact. He dropped them into the bottom of the boat where they flopped around a bit, then lay still. Then he re-baited the hooks and shoved off again.

After checking four more trout lines, they had a total of nine catfish. Walter said they'd check the lines again later that afternoon, and headed the boat back home. Once there, he dropped the fish into a bucket of water and returned to his seat on the porch. Mary took her place beside him, and the two rocked silently together. Billy sat beside Melissa and held her hand. She laid her head on his shoulder.

"Is Thad your son?" Billy asked after a while.

Walter and Mary looked at each other for a long moment. The sadness in their eyes made Billy regret asking the question.

"No, sir. Thaddeus is our grandson," Walter said softly. "The government, they took his father. He got killed in the war." Mary patted the back of his hand tenderly. "They sent us this medal in his place." Walter unfolded a handkerchief from his pocket and handed an object to Billy.

"This is a Congressional Medal of Honor!" Billy gushed. "Your son must have been a hero."

"That's what they said," Walter stated flatly.

"I never was able to join the military," Billy said when Walter offered no further details.

"Neither me."

"I always felt like I missed out on something."

"You didn't."

"It just seems like a noble sacrifice, putting your life on the line to protect truth and justice."

"Dead is dead." Walter's face turned solemn. "Some things a man has got to fight for. Some things a man has got to die for. But most times, it's all just bullshit."

Billy handed the medal back to Walter with near religious awe, as if he were handing him a bloodstained nail from the cross of Christ. Walter wrapped it up in the cloth and replaced it in his pocket. He turned his gaze out over the water and continued rocking.

"We'll check the lines again a little later, then we'll take 'em up to Mrs. Brown's store."

CHAPTER 24

❦

Stephen straightened his back against his chair, planted his feet firmly on the floor, and clenched his teeth. The more he listened to his brother, the tighter he clutched the phone.

"In other words," he spat into the tiny cellular device, "she got away, right? Is that what you're trying to tell me? And that idiot and his men killed two cops?" he continued, his voice escalating. "There were supposed to be six of them!" Stephen finished in a shout. "How could she get away?"

He listened again, then chopped at the air as if the other party could see him gesture and the fury on his face. "Well, that's just great!" Stephen raged. "Just great! The cops'll be watching that place like a hawk now. We can't even send someone in to find out what happened to them, or if they ran, or where they went." He growled under his breath for a moment, then slammed his palm on the desk. "Now you listen up, you little twerp, and you listen good, understand? You take care of them, understand?" Stephen snapped. "Let your buddy David do it. The one you keep telling me can walk on water."

He listened again, and waved away the argument. "Ah, I don't care! Then get someone else! Jesus! I can't believe those stupid idiots would shoot a New Orleans cop. That's worse than assassinating the President, for Christ's sake!"

He started to hang up, then called into the phone, "Wait! I've only dealt with Jon," he said a little more calmly, as though he had found a beacon of light in an otherwise dark tunnel. "No one else should know who I am."

Stephen took in a deep breath of air as he listened, held it for a few seconds, and exhaled sharply. "This has already gotten out of hand. It was supposed to be a quiet, simple operation, and now it's a fiasco. We've got fliers all over creation, two dead cops, and a direct line back to me sitting in the jailhouse." He lowered his head and rubbed his temples with his thumb and forefinger, trying to think. "I want this straightened out now, understand? Or I swear by all that's holy…" Stephen stopped himself and took a deep breath. "Get back to me as soon as you know something."

Stephen clicked the button on his phone and slipped it back into his pocket. He felt the pressure starting to build, a bubbling urgency somewhere deep inside. He knew it would continue to grow and stress him out until he had the situation under control. He kicked the door several times leaving black scuffmarks on the white finish.

Jon had handled himself well during the police interrogation. He'd managed to not let anything vital slip. As of yet, as far as he knew, no one even suspected why he and his "friends" had gone to the bar. He had taken on the cops' best, and prevailed. They had pressed every available button—guilt, sympathy, even "good cop/bad cop", all to no avail; he'd beaten them every time, never giving in or giving up. He knew if he talked it would not only mean the end of his professional career, but probably his life as well. But he also knew he hadn't been the one that pulled the trigger on either of those dead men in the car. He probably wouldn't end up doing more then a few years, with time off for good behavior. If he greased the right palms, he might even get a mistrial, especially since he appeared as a first-time offender. This was the first job that had ever gone wrong; he had no police record.

As soon as the judge set bail, his lawyer would see to an immediate release. His lawyer was on a $15,000-a-year retainer; time to cash-in that insurance policy.

Roy walked toward G-man's desk with a box of donuts.
"Have you heard?" he asked.
"Yeah," G-man sighed. "Real shame. Two fine boys."
Roy nodded his agreement. "Billy and the girl got away."
"That's good."
The two men sat across from each other, each lost in his own thoughts. Both knew it was senseless to try and comfort the other. Nothing could make either of them feel less guilty about the two young cops who had died doing them a favor. They hadn't even died in the line of duty—they were just doing a favor for a friend. Of course, enough strings would be pulled to ensure that the widows would get the maximum insurance and benefits, but that was little consolation. Like putting a Band-Aid on a headache, it made everything look better, but it did nothing for the pain. The collection they had started for the widows already contained nine thousand dollars, but it, too, did little to soothe either man's savage guilt.
"I was hoping I'd get to talk with the dirt bags," Roy said.
"They've been in interrogation all day. None of them has budged yet. The good news is, no judge is going to let them out on bail. I can probably get you in to see them in a couple of days, as soon as everything cools off a bit."
"I just want to know for sure who sent them."
"Well, my money is on Mr. Pruit."
"I'm pretty sure of that myself."
G-man drummed his fingers on a blank slip of paper. "You know, that takes your boy's game to a new level. A dangerous level."
"Yeah, and I'm not even sure where they are. I know they're hiding, but where, I can't even begin to guess."

"Maybe we should go have a talk with kingfish Pruit himself. Move this game to the home court." G-man smiled slightly, and looked at Roy through the corner of his eye. "Know what I mean?"

"I was already thinking about that…. You shouldn't go, though. I'm a civilian. It would be less complicated if I went alone."

G-man grimaced, but nodded. The police force had so many rules about when and why an officer could question someone that things could get tricky pretty quick. Although not an official cop, G-man did work in the police department. Best to keep everything as unofficial as possible—especially for what they planned.

Roy slid the box of donuts across the desk like a briefcase full of small unmarked bills. "I need the address," he said quietly.

G-man smiled. "You know I hate donuts."

"I know. I just thought it might be funny. I knew you'd be in the dumps."

"Thanks. You could have at least brought coffee, too."

G-man picked up the paper his hand had been resting on, glanced at the underside, and handed it to Roy. "You know I'm always two steps ahead of you.

Roy chuckled grimly. "Thanks."

"No problem. Just remember, you didn't get it from me."

"Get what?"

"Exactly."

Roy smiled and walked away.

Anderson sat opposite his brother in a high-back leather chair, his briefcase on the floor beside him. He crossed his legs. "I've been in touch with Jon's lawyer," he said. "I think we may be able to work something out."

"Like what?"

"He's been petitioning the court all morning to set bail. I got in touch with him through a third party, and found out he's pretty unhappy with his client, anyway. If he defends somebody that everyone thinks is a cop killer, he's going to do himself more long-term damage than good. He's ready to wash his hands of the whole thing."

"Okay. And…?"

"I told him that a certain anonymous party wants his client to leave the country. But you're going to have to repay whatever bail he loses."

"Yeah, whatever."

"David may be willing to put in a call to a contact at the DA's office. If we can get the DA to put in a call to the judge, we may be able to get bail set relatively quick and inexpensively. Well, inexpensive for an accused cop killer anyway. You just have to make sure they're never seen again."

Stephen shook his head. "This is all too much trouble. Just kill him."

"Are you sure?"

Stephen nodded slightly.

"Ok."

The intercom buzzed. "Yeah, what is it?"

"There's a gentleman here to see you, sir."

"About what?" Stephen demanded.

"He said he has some information about Mrs. Pruit."

"Send him in." He sat back in his chair. "This could be good."

Anderson tilted his head. "Be very careful. Those guys could have already talked to the cops. Whoever this is, he could be here to rattle the cage a bit."

After a few minutes, the butler stuck his head in. "A Mr. LeBlanc to see you, sir."

"That's fine. Show him in."

Roy marched straight up to the desk and stared directly into Stephen's eyes.

Stephen stood and extended his hand. "Stephen Pruit," he said with a smile, ignoring the contempt in Roy's set jaw and hard expression.

"I know," Roy said dryly. He glanced at the out stretched hand, then sat down without saying a word. Stephen retracted his hand and sat.

"I understand you have some information about my wife, Mr. LeBlanc."

"More than you'd like for me to have."

"Excuse me?" Stephen said, his bright smile fading a bit.

Roy's narrowed his eyes and let his countenance get dark. "I know about the money, her father, and the contract."

Stephen shifted in his seat. "I'm not sure what you're talking about."

Anderson perched uneasily on his seat, waiting for the opportunity to be a lawyer, but not sure what he could say that wouldn't somehow get him into trouble.

"I know you were holding her prisoner here. My guess is, you'd found some loophole you were going to make her sign the money over to you, somehow. Once her signature was on the paper, you were going to kill her."

Anderson cleared his throat. "Excuse me, sir, but are you a police officer? Are you here in an official capacity?"

Roy turned his head slowly and made a cop's snap judgement on the speaker. "Nope," he said, using his most belittling look and sarcastic voice. "I used to be, but now I'm just a civilian here on a friendly visit. And, just between you and me, friend, you had better watch your step."

"Is this something Melissa told you?" Stephen put in. He was aware of how quickly his brother had shriveled under the man's gaze. "The girl is unstable you know," he offered.

Roy turned back to him. "Yeah, she told me about you. She didn't seem all that unstable to me. More scared out of her mind. But that's not why I'm here."

Stephen leaned back in his chair and placed his fingertips together under his chin. "Why are you here? Money?"

"Oh, no, Mr. Pruit. I don't have any children…"

Stephen licked his lips. It occurred to him that the man might be crazy. He smiled slightly. "So?"

"So," Roy continued. "I came here to tell you that the man your wife is with is the closest thing I will ever have to a son."

Stephen said nothing. Roy let his face take on a look of studied forbearance. "He's not interested in your money, and neither is she. They just want you to leave them alone."

"Well," Stephen said, "if what she told you were true, you'd know it isn't that simple."

"Maybe not." Roy smiled, but not pleasantly. "But let me give you something simple. Some simple truth."

"Okay."

"I know every cop in New Orleans. I know every judge. I know every law-enforcement official. These people are all friends of mine. Everyone one of them. So it's this simple: if you harm that boy, I will kill you."

"Mr. LeBlanc! Is that a threat?"

"No, sir, no, sir. It's the God's honest truth. Harm the boy and I'll kill you. It's a simple fact."

Anderson bolted out of his chair. "I don't know who you think you are, but I could file charges on you for even saying that!"

"You be my guest. Just remember what I just said." Roy stood, nodded, and walked out, slamming the door behind him.

Stephen flashed Anderson a look of concern, then pressed the intercom button to the guardhouse.

"Yes, Sir?"

"Did you take down our visitor's plate number?"

"Yes sir, and logged him in at 11:12 a.m."

"Good. Get the information to Jay and ask him to come to my office."

"Yes sir."

Anderson sat down. "This certainly complicates things."

Stephen repeatedly tapped the desk with his fingers. "I am going to have Jay run the plate and find out who the guy is. We'll know more after that."

"You want me to have him arrested?"

"No!" Stephen snapped. "If he's telling the truth he'd be out in an hour, if they even bothered to lock him up. We'll have the whole world watching us. Let's just wait and see what develops."

"All right," Anderson said. "In the meantime, I'm going to get back on the cop killers. You're getting more fires getting started than I can put out," he whined.

"Oh shut up! Just handle one at a time—even you should be able to do that. The first order of business is to get those idiots out of jail, and get that fire doused."

Anderson nodded and picked up his briefcase. "Give me a call as soon as you know what's up with that guy."

"It shouldn't take more than a couple of hours. When do we deal with Jon?"

"I'll get on it right away."

"Hire the best. I want this straightened out ASAP, and I don't care what you have to do. Just handle it."

"David knows the right people, we've even got a cop on the inside, but it'll cost you," warned Anderson.

"I don't care. Just make sure that whoever does it gets all the information they can first. If Jon knows anything we need it."

"I'll get on it right now."

"When can you get back to me?"

"Early afternoon."

"Good. Call me when."

Anderson stood and looked at his watch. "I have a lunch scheduled with David; I don't want to be late."

Stephen gestured angrily; Anderson left the office.

Stephen leaned his chair back as far as it would go and rubbed his temples again, but the panic in his stomach only grew stronger and more unyielding. He thrust the chair forward, ground his teeth, and tried to slow his breathing, but the pressure in his chest flared like a rapidly spreading forest fire. If he did anything rash, he could mess up everything he had worked for over the last few years. He would simply have to deal with it, and wait.

He hated waiting!

CHAPTER 25

Jon sat up on the side of his bunk when he heard the guard open the door to take the prisoners to breakfast. He stood at the door of his tiny cell and waited for the guard to walk down the tier and open each door individually. Prisoners could not touch the doors until they all were unlocked, and the guard gave the command. On order they opened their doors and stepped into the hall to form a single-file line. The cell doors stayed open while they ate so the guards could search them, if they so desired.

The guard gave the command and the line started its slow march to the chow hall. Once there, each prisoner picked up a tray and a spoon—knives and forks were not allowed—and walked sideways along the mess line while other prisoners slapped the daily course on their individual metal trays. Today's delight consisted of dry toast and unsalted hash browns, better named wilted hash blacks. Each inmate received one cup of watered-down coffee and a plastic container of orange juice. Jon shuffled his way through the line, slid into his place at a table, and began to eat.

After breakfast, they led him back to his cell and locked him up again. After his third morning in jail, he wondered what could possibly be taking his lawyer so long to free him. He had been beaten and mentally tortured. The cops kept calling him a cop killer, even though he hadn't pulled the trigger—something he'd started repeating, almost continuously, sometime during the second day of "questioning." Jon felt lucky to be alive. He was the only one of the six in this cellblock; the rest of his men were still laid up in the infirmary with varying degrees of injury.

The day passed slowly. He stared at the wall for a while, then at the ceiling. When he became bored with that, he stared at the wall again. At least they weren't going to "question" him today.

Jon spent the night tossing and turning, unable to fall completely asleep. Lack of exercise had made him restless; his mind raced a million miles a second. Sometime around 3:00 a.m., he heard footsteps and muffled voices coming down the hall. They stopped out side of his cell.

"Him?" one of the voices whispered.

"Yeah," the other answered. "Keep it quiet, but find out what he knows."

The cell door opened and a prisoner stepped in.

"Hey, what's going on?" Jon demanded.

The prisoner was on him in a flash. "Shut up," he snapped. He trapped Jon from behind in a one-armed bear hug and pressed the point of a knife against Jon's throat.

"I'll be back," the guard whispered. Then he was gone.

"We need to talk," the new prisoner breathed into Jon's ear.

Jon nodded, but only slightly. He didn't want to cut himself. A few seconds later, Jon heard the hall door close and lock.

CHAPTER 26

Roy sat at a corner table in Tujagues Restaurant next to Jackson Square for over 20 minutes waiting on G-man. The two were meeting for lunch to discuss their options. Roy was more worried about Billy than anything else, but he knew G-man's focus was strictly on revenge. He was the one who had personally asked the favor from the two rookies, and had even leaned on them a little to get the answer he wanted. Their funerals were set for tomorrow at three in the afternoon. Roy wondered how he and G-man would handle facing the grieving widows.

Roy shifted his weight and looked at his watch. It was unusual for his friend to run this late, but then, in the Big Easy, anything could have held him up. Roy could not number all the times some unexpected parade or a Creole funeral marching down the middle of the street—complete with jazz band and an ensemble of dancers—had delayed him. He sipped at his water and scanned the daily menu. A unique restaurant, Tujagues employed four chefs, each cooking one of their specialties every day. Customers could choose from any of the four. No one ever complained about the lack of other choices, because the talented chefs produced truly unique dishes, and the food tasted incredible. Each table displayed a small laminated card with the restaurant's history and the amazing fact that Tujagues had survived Prohibition with only three bartenders.

Roy leaned back in his seat, lifting the chair's two front legs off the floor, and let his thoughts wander.

"Sir, are you ready to order?"

"Huh?" Roy looked up, startled. "Oh, sorry. Just bring me an Abita Amber for now," he said. He glanced at his watch again. He'd wait a little longer.

A few seconds later the waiter returned with the ice-cold beer and a frosty mug. Roy picked up the beer and drank straight from the bottle. He had half finished it when G-man walked in the door.

"About time!"

G-man sat down with a grimace.

"Everything okay?"

"He's dead," G-man said dryly.

"What do you mean?"

"The cop killer. He's dead."

"How? What happened?" Roy shifted to the edge of his seat.

"Found in his cell this morning with his throat cut. By the time I heard about it and got someone down there, they'd already cleaned up. No one heard anything."

Roy leaned forward. "You know what that means," he said.

"Yeah, they're desperate," G-man nodded. He furrowed his brow and he looked down at the table. "I'm sorry, man," he whispered.

Roy was silent for a moment. Finally, he shrugged. "Don't worry about it. I shook Pruit up enough the other day. He'll make a mistake."

"I surely hope so."

"What about the other men?" Roy asked after a pause.

G-man shook his head. "They don't know anything…."

"…or they're not talking," Roy finished the sentence.

"Exactly."

"When do they get out of the infirmary?"

"One of them is out already. They've got him downtown now, but everyone knows what they did, and everyone knows they're after Billy—-I knew that was coming. I can get us a private interview."

"When?" Roy said.

"Give me a few hours." G-man showed the barest of smiles. "I'll have one of our boys set it up."

"Make sure they don't file it," Roy said. "Keep it low profile."

G-man's smile turned into a big grin. "You got it."

Eric Zimmer left his cell and followed the guard to a room in the back of the building with a metal table and three chairs in the center. It looked just like any other holding room except for the missing two-way glass. The guard nodded at the cop perched on the edge of the table, pushed Eric farther into the room, and left.

Without a word, the cop motioned Eric to sit and handcuffed his hands behind his back. Then he started to tie Eric's legs to the chair with leather straps.

"Hey, what's this about?" the thug asked.

"Shut up."

"You know I have a lawyer?"

"You know your friend had his throat cut last night?"

Eric paled. "Which one?"

"Jon-Jon," the guard smiled.

Eric swallowed hard. "Look I didn't have…."

"Shut up!"

The cop finished strapping Eric to the chair and left. Eric sat bound and alone for what seemed like hours until, at length, the cop returned with two other men. One had a small plastic trash bag. Despite himself, Eric's heart began to pound. He had seen several people die with just that kind of small plastic trash bag tied around their heads to cut off their air. He'd often wondered why the people did not just bite a hole in the bag and breath. He didn't want to die, but if that's what it took to protect his friends, then that's what he would do. He knew if he told the cops what they wanted to know his "associates" would kill him for sure. His only leverage was in holding onto what little information he had; maybe he could at least bargain.

One man sat in the chair directly across the table from Eric. The other man sat to his left. The uniformed cop resumed his earlier position on the edge of the table.

"We have a few questions for you," said the man in the middle, making no small show of the bag.

"I don't have nothing to say to you," Eric responded with as much show of disdain as he could. He tried not to let his eyes land on the plastic bag.

"Do you know what this is?" The man held up a large can of pepper mace.

"Yeah. So?"

The man pulled on a pair of disposable gloves, shook open the bag, and sprayed a liberal amount of the pepper spray inside. He clenched the top shut in his fist.

"Now, this won't kill you," he said, shaking the bag slowly, "but it will make you talk. I want to know more about Stephen Pruit."

Eric almost laughed with relief. "I ain't talking to you. You can't scare me with that lousy little spray. You'll have to do better than that! Pepper's for women, man. Scares away muggers and dogs! It ain't no real weapon."

"Oh, so you've experienced it before?"

He answered before he could stop himself. "Yeah." He mentally shrugged and decided to play it out. "Yeah, so I been sprayed before, what of it? Sure it hurt, but only for a little while. You don't scare me," he repeated.

The man with the bag stepped closer. "I'll give you one chance to change your mind."

"You're not getting anything out of me."

G-man shrugged at Roy, who nodded, then slipped the bag over Eric's head.

Eric felt like his head was engulfed in flames. He grabbed at the bag with his teeth to try and bite through it, but all that did was cover his lips and gums with pepper spray and suck a great gulp of it down his throat. He tried to throw himself away but the cop was holding the back of the chair. He jerked his head around, coughing, gagging. He couldn't move, couldn't get away from it. His stomach was searing, the fire spreading down into his intestines. After an eternity of several seconds, the bag came off. He started crying and promptly vomited into his own lap.

"I am going to sue you guys!" Eric shouted.

All three men burst out laughing. Roy sprayed more pepper into the bag, and slipped it over his head for a few seconds then removed it.

"We were after the girl!" Eric gasped between gulps of clean air. "They got away! I didn't kill the cop, it was George! George did it! It was his idea!" Eric slobbered on about everything he had done wrong since the third grade.

Roy glanced at G-man, who just shook his head with a barely repressed smile. It never failed to amaze him how easily a lung-full of pepper spray could break through anybody's resistance.

In the end, they learned everything they could from Eric except for that which he did not know: who had hired them, why the job was so urgent, and where Billy and the girl had fled. They made him clean up the holding room then sent him back to his cell.

"Well, that was useless," G-man finally said, as he slowly tied up the used bag and his discarded gloves in another plastic sack.

"We could talk to that other guy, George," the cop offered.

"What's the point?" Roy countered. "He wouldn't know anything more than this guy. I'm afraid the only one who could give us anything is the one we didn't get to fast enough. We're no better off than we were before."

"Motor-1, outstanding." Stephen clapped his hands. "That shouldn't take long."

"David's already made contact with a friend from the DMV. It's just a matter of time." Anderson sounded somewhat smug. "Assuming of course the bike's registered in his name. We'll track him down and…"

"Well, time is the one thing I don't have a lot of." Stephen cut in. "Did Jon say anything else?"

"Nothing useful. The convict said he was trying to pray when he died."

"Really, hmm. I guess you can never tell what a person will do in his last few moments."

"I guess that's true." Anderson eyed Stephen. "Just relax. Let me find this guy for you then we'll move on with the plan."

CHAPTER 27

Stephen leaned back in his chair and propped his feet on the corner of his desk. Anderson sprawled in the chair across from him, his eyes fluttering open every few seconds as he stopped himself from falling asleep. Several other men were still milling around the office, which was strewn with dozens of different Louisiana maps. They'd been looking for any trace of a town named "Alligator Bayou." So far, they'd come up empty.

"I'm really getting tired of this," Stephen yawned, rubbing his eyes. "Too much stress. I hardly slept two hours last night. Are you sure it's Alligator Bayou?"

Anderson nodded. "Why don't you just stay here and get some rest? Let these guys go look for her. We'll find the town, I mean-it's listed on the records of the DMV –it's got to be here somewhere."

"No, I'm going myself," Stephen sighed. "Things are already screwed up enough. It's already cost me close to a million bucks to take care of Jon and his idiots. Every time I let someone else get involved it creates another potential problem. No way in hell am I going to be the richest man on the cell block."

"Well, I wish you the best of luck." Anderson glanced at his watch and stood up. "I've got a lunch with David."

"Yeah, whatever," Stephen grumbled.

Stephen watched his brother leave before tilting his head back and closing his eyes. He wanted this done quickly, quietly, and with no further delays. Time was fast becoming the enemy. The pressure of not knowing where his wife was or what she was planning seemed to double with every tick of the clock. The last few nights, Stephen had awakened from terrifying dreams and found himself in a cold sweat. Panic attacks were hitting at untimely intervals, stressing him into in the foulest of moods. By now, he'd given up his plans to get even with the freak: LeBlanc's story had checked out, and Stephen took the threat seriously. Civilians could run all over the police in Chicago, New York, or Los Angeles, where ex-cops were nothing more than a joke, but Louisiana was a different story. Here, the cops and judicial system stuck together for better or worse, and no one even pretended they always served on the side of the law. Stephen wasn't about to push his luck with the old man. Still, $80,000,000—free and clear—would go a long way toward helping him ignore the scar across his face. Hell, he could have the thing fixed by a good plastic surgeon. Besides, he tried to convince himself for the hundredth time, revenge was highly overrated.

"I found it," Jay call out joyfully. "Just outside Baton Rouge. This is the only map that even has it listed."

"Good job," Stephen mumbled. "Put yourself down for a cigar." Stephen yawned and rubbed his eyes. "Get the guys ready to go. I am going to try to take a nap."

"Yes sir," Jon nodded to Stephen's back as he walked out of the room.

By 10:00 a.m., the limo waited to carry three men plus Stephen to Alligator Bayou near Baton Rouge. They would start by simply asking questions, handing out a little money. Stephen was sure he'd find Melissa near the capital city, plotting some kind of evil scheme against him. He would not allow her to succeed.

The men stood near the car comparing maps and discussing the best route while Stephen finalized preparations in the house. At 10:30 on the dot, he walked out of the house.

The men scurried about trying to appear busy. Stephen strode to the rear door and waited. Jay gave the driver a threatening look, sending him into a trot around the rear of the car to open Mr. Pruit's door.

Stephen slid into the rear of the limo and did a quick inventory of the bar to verify it was fully stocked and had plenty of ice. He checked the TV/VCR combo and the videotape selection before flipping on a soap opera.

Outside, Jay supervised as one of his men packed Stephen's four large suitcases and everyone else's small overnight bags. Finally, Jay got in next to the driver, and the other three climbed into the middle section of the limo, closed off from Stephen's roomier, luxury compartment by an electric, privacy glass window.

They took off at 10:45 under a cloudless sky, and soon hit a stretch of intersection filled with overgrown jungle and swampland. A few small towns stood back from the highway. A new outlet mall packed with bargain hunters was the scenery highlight. Ragged people wearing old tattered clothing sat with fishing poles at nearly every bridge or body of water, trying their luck for the day. Stephen found it amusing to think they might actually be out there trying to catch their evening meal. He eyed the small cabins with their fronts hanging over the water that showed through at every spot where the trees parted enough to see the swamp. The boats tied to porches and little docks took the place of cars parked in a driveway.

While the men talked quietly among themselves, the driver followed the highlighted lines on his map, double-checking it after he had turned onto a deserted gravel road that appeared to lead to nowhere. After several confusing turns and a few miles of nothingness, he pulled up to a small community next to the swamp sporting a hand-painted sign: "Alligator Bayou."

Only two buildings were visible; one appeared to be a store/bait shop, the other a bar. Nearby trailers rested nearly 20 feet off the ground on stilts. Several pirogues and a few flat-bottom aluminum boats bobbed on the water. A number of people were in sight, all carrying either some type of fishing equipment or a stringer of fish.

Stephen looked around and tapped the intercom. "This can't be it, can it?" he said.

"If you were wanting to hide, this could be paradise," Jay's voice came back.

"Hmm."

The long white limo eased to a stop in front of the General Store. Barefoot, unwashed, rotten-toothed children gawked through half-open eyes at the big shiny car, their mouths hanging open, some actually drooling.

The gang of children flocked around Jay as he got out of the car and walked toward the store. Wordlessly, they stayed on his heels until he started to climb the steps. They stared up at him silently from the foot of the stairs, each waiting to see if a sad face and pleading look would pay off with some candy or a treat from the rich man.

In the meantime, the adults in the area all watched the limo with undisguised suspicion bordering on hostility. They were not used to strangers and made no pretense of welcoming them. Theirs was a society more exclusive than the finest country clubs, and the only way to gain admittance was through the trust of a member, hard to come by in the small community. He knew his expensive clothes and fancy car did not impress these people. In fact, they were just things to resent, things that drew a definite line of separation between "us" and "them." The 'thems' were never welcome.

Mrs. Brown looked warily at the man who had entered her store. His suit had to have cost more than her building and all its contents. She folded her arms under her frown and waited.

"Good afternoon. My name is Jay."

She nodded slightly.

"I was wondering if you could help me?" Jay paused, hoping the woman would ask what he needed. When she didn't, he continued. "We were looking for someone...."

"Ain't seen 'em," she cut him off gruffly.

"Well, it's a woman and a man with a scarred..."

"Ain't seen 'em," she insisted.

"Just hear me out," Jay tried, flashing a smile.

"I'm busy."

"There is a substantial reward..."

"Ain't seen 'em!" she said sharply. She set her face into an even harder frown and moved her hands to her hips. "Ain't seen 'em, ain't going to. I'm busy. You buyin' something?"

"I see," Jay said. "Well, have a nice day." He backed out of the door, turned toward the stairs and stopped suddenly. The children were still waiting, motionless, their heads cocked back, their mouths flopped open. He wasn't absolutely sure they weren't cannibals sizing up their next meal. He quickly made his way back to the car, slid in next to Stephen, and locked the door. The children cast longing glances over their shoulders as they filtered away.

Stephen looked at Jay and waited for an answer. "Well," he asked impatiently?

"The woman won't talk," Jay said. "I get the feeling she may be hiding something, but there's no way to know."

Stephen gave a short laugh. He had expected as much. "Well let's stake out the area for a few days and see if we can get the people to loosen up a bit, we'll find someone," he said. "Hand out a little money. She's here, she'll turn up."

"How do you know she's here?"

Stephen nodded toward the side of the store. "Motor-1," Stephen mumbled.

Jon craned his neck around and saw the license plate on the back of a motorcycle. "Well, can't argue with that."

Stephen instructed the driver to park between two large fishing boats among the house trailers to help the big car blend in and look less threatening. Then he settled back in his seat, fixed himself a drink, and silently toasted the unknown informant he knew lurked in every ragged community like this—the guy who would to sell his soul for the right amount of money. The guy so desperate to get out, he'd break all the rules, shatter the code, destroy the inner circle. The guy…just like him.

CHAPTER 28

❁

Mrs. Brown gazed out the screen door and studied the intruders. The men shifted in their seats, leaned against the car, and generally appeared to annoy one another. They watched as people came and went from the store, and approached most of them. As of yet no one seemed willing to talk. Most only nodded and continued on their way.

Rolling her nails across the counter, Mrs. Brown looked from the men to the bayou landing dock. Walter and Billy would be coming around the corner with the day's catch at any time now. She glanced back at the men, then scanned the area looking for someone to send as a messenger.

She quickly spotted Rick Burrows, but continued to look around, trying to fight off the sinking feeling that she would have to rely on him. "Oh, no," she moaned aloud. No one else was available.

Rick had never been a bad child, just shifty. He had joined the Marine Corps the year before, but they shipped him back home in short order, calling him undesirable or unfit for military service. Since then, he had generally bullied and bossed anyone he could, boasted of his purported military exploits, and appeared to be generally up to no good most of the time. A lot of the folks around were convinced he even poached fish from their lines and traps. Mrs.

Brown came around from behind the counter and opened the screen door onto the porch.

"Richard?" She waved her hand in the air. "Richard!"

He looked up at her, glanced over his shoulder to see if she was talking to someone else, then turned back and pointed his index finger at his chest.

She nodded and motioned him over.

He put down his bucket and tackle box and headed in her direction.

"Yes, ma'am?"

"Richard, I need you to do me a favor."

"Sure." He smiled, yet his tone sounded slightly annoyed.

"I need you to go out to Walter and Mary's house and tell them not to bring their fish in for a few days."

"Well, won't his fish spoil?"

"Don't worry about that. Those men over there—don't look," she added quickly, but too late. "Look at me. They're here looking for some people staying at Walter's house and offering money for information." She immediately wished she had not said anything about money. "You need to make sure Walter knows about them."

"What would they want with anyone out here?"

"Don't worry about that, just do what I ask."

Rick looked back over his shoulder again."

"Stop looking. You'll draw their attention." She noticed two of the men had turned to watch them. "Now, see what you did."

"They cops?"

"No. Now, you be sure to go by Walter's lines and see if you find them out there. You know where his lines are?"

"Yeah." He nodded, then paused. "At least I...I think so."

"Well, go now. And hurry. And don't tell nobody."

He nodded and walked away, casting several glances toward the car.

"Stupid boy," she mumbled, her hands grasping at each other as she walked back into the store. She watched through the window as Rick tossed a few things into his boat and pushed it off the bank into the water. He jumped in, sat down in the rear, grabbed the pull cord on the motor, and gave it a coupled of hard pulls. He turned up the gas and the motor sputtered to life. He put it in gear and started to ease forward, then looked toward the car, and waved timidly.

"Darn you, Richard Burrows," Mrs. Brown muttered through clenched teeth.

Billy came out of the cabin and sat on the porch with his back against the wall. Walter was rocking back and forth in his chair. "Soon as we eat, we'll go check the lines, maybe have a couple of cool ones."

Billy smiled. "Sounds good to me." They had only been here for a couple of days, but he had already fallen into the routine of going out with Walter during the days, and spending the evenings and nights snuggled with Melissa. Just as he was thinking how pleasant things had turned out, Melissa came out of the house onto the porch. He reached up to take her and pull her down to his lap. He put his arms around her and kissed her gently on the cheek before moving his lips to her ear.

"Angel face," he whispered. She smiled and laid her head back on his shoulder.

"Who's that?" she asked suddenly.

"Who? What do you mean?"

"I hear someone coming."

Billy listened. He could faintly make out the sound of an approaching boat motor. He instantly tensed. "Are you expecting anyone?" he asked Walter.

Walter shook his head. "We never expecting nobody, but sometimes people just show up."

Billy eased himself and Melissa to their feet. "Go inside with Mary."

"What's wrong? Is everything ok?"

"I'm sure it's nothing. Just go inside. I'd rather have you out of sight."

"Ashamed of me already?" She showed a halfhearted smile. He kissed her cheek.

"It'll be ok, I promise," he said. He squeezed her hand. "Go ahead, go on in."

"Maybe both of you ought to go on in for a bit," Walter put in. "I'll see who this is."

"Ok," Billy agreed. "I'll just be inside if you need any help."

Walter chuckled. "Boy I been out here longer than you been alive. I don't need no help."

Billy chuckled. "I believe that."

He walked Melissa into the cabin and stood just beyond the window so he could look out without being seen.

Presently, a fishing boat rounded the corner and sped toward Walter's boat landing, heading straight toward the mud bank. The driver gunned the motor, then tilted it forward, lifting the propeller out of the water. The boat's speed pushed it about halfway onto the bank, bringing it to rest beside Walter's. A young man jumped out, waved at Walter with a "Hey!" and started toward the cabin.

"Howdy son," Walter responded. "What can I do for you?"

"Well, sir, Ms. Brown sent me here to tell you something." He stopped and waited.

"Well, what is it, son?"

"She said some rich men were here, well, up at the store, looking for somebody staying with you."

Melissa gasped aloud and leaned back into Billy's arms. "Oh my God, Billy!"

"Shush," Billy whispered. He kissed the top of her head and hugged her tightly. "It'll be ok."

The young man had apparently heard her because he concentrated his stare at the window for a long moment.

"Is that right?" Walter was saying. "Anything else?"

"Yes, sir. She said not to bring your fish up there for awhile."

"Umm-hum. Well, I'll be. Well, thank you, son."

"No problem. Anything I can do to help?"

"Oh, I don't believe so, but thanks, anyway."

"Yes, sir." Richard started to back away, staring first at Walter, then at the window. "Glad I could help."

"Well, thanks, again."

He backed up a few more steps, then turned to walk to the boat. He searched the window from over his shoulder as he pushed the craft into the water, then climbed on board. He soon disappeared around the bend.

Melissa stood silently tears welling in her eyes. Billy snuggled his face into her neck and rested his chin on her tiny shoulder.

"It's ok, baby. It's ok. Don't worry, Angel Face, I'm not going to let anything happen to you."

"I know," she whispered. "But what about you?"

"Don't worry about me."

She pressed her cheek against his chest. "Promise me," she said, her voice quivering with emotion. "Promise you won't get yourself hurt trying to protect me. He can't kill me, Billy."

"I know."

"Promise me."

"Baby, I'm not going…" He took a breath. "I'm not going to let him hurt you."

"No, Billy, no! You've got to promise! He can't do anything to me, but he can hurt you. And he's mean, Billy, he's real mean. He can hurt you bad."

"Okay, well…look, let's make sure we know what's going on before we jump to conclusions. Maybe it's not even him."

"You know it's him."

"Maybe. And maybe it's the same guys as before."

Billy moved toward the door, still holding Melissa. He pushed the door open with his foot. Mary reached around to hold it open and follow them out.

"You all right, baby?" she asked, placing a gentle hand on Melissa's shoulder.

Melissa nodded bravely, but Billy could feel her trembling.

"That was pretty fast," Walter said. "They must be really desperate to get her back."

"I'm sure they are."

"I hope Thadious is all right."

"So do I."

"Well, I guess now we have to decide what to do." Walter rocked slowly in his chair. Mary settled into hers and began to rock. Billy and Melissa slid down to their customary place against the wall, holding onto each other as if for dear life.

Billy's jaw muscles soon began to ache from clenching his teeth while his thoughts raced through endless scenarios of escape and capture. He wouldn't allow Melissa to be torn from him, but he had to be careful not to act rashly. Sometimes moving too quickly could turn out worse than not moving at all. The pleasant air of just a few moments ago was gone. Now all he felt was an evil darkness lurking in the background, waiting for a chance to strike.

CHAPTER 29

Her arms folded across her chest, Mrs. Brown stood at the store window watching Rick furtively eyeing the limo while pretending to be busy with his boat. Finally, he leaned against the boat and stared at the car for a moment, then waved. One of the men waved back and started walking toward him.

Mrs. Brown rushed out the door in time to catch Rick taking his first few steps toward the approaching man.

"Richard Burrows!" she shouted from the front of the store. "Come here a minute."

He paused, glanced at the man, then walked slowly to the front of the store.

"How come you ain't gone to check your fish traps yet?" Mrs. Brown questioned. "You know, the guy from Baton Rouge is going to be here in a bit to pick them up. If you don't have them here, I can't sell them for you."

"Yes, ma'am."

She waited, but when he didn't move, she got angry. "Well, boy? You want to get paid this week?"

"Yes, ma'am," he mumbled. He walked slowly back toward his boat. Then he stopped and glanced at the man.

"Go on now!" she half shouted.

"Yes, ma'am." He pushed his boat into the water and climbed aboard.

Now I got to find someone else to warn Walter, she thought, watching the boat leave the shore. I should never have trusted that Rick Burrows. He's gonna be back soon, and blamed if he won't just tell those men anything they want to know. Maybe I ought to go myself. At least it would give me a chance to apologize.

Stephen watched the young man float away on his boat, glancing back over his shoulder at them. Jay returned to the car.

"He knows something," Stephen said.

Jay agreed. "I'd be willing to bet on it."

"When he comes back, get next to him and bring him over here. Let's get this mess behind us."

"Yes, sir."

Walter and Mary held hands and rocked. Melissa sat on the floor, her back against the wall, hugging her knees to her chest. But Billy couldn't sit any longer. He paced back and forth across the porch, nervously rubbing his palms together and watching the shoreline.

"It sure didn't take long for him to find us," he said.

"I told you he was very determined," Melissa almost whimpered. "I knew he would find us. Now we've put Walter and Mrs. Mary in danger!"

"Child, don't you worry about us none," Mary interjected. "I've got my man to take care of me." She patted Walter on the knee. Walter simply nodded. He never missed a rock.

"Do you think they know where we are?" Billy fretted. "I mean here, at this house?"

"If he doesn't know now, he will soon," Melissa said. "He'll either bully, intimidate, or pay someone for the information, just like he found out about the bar, just like he found out about this place. He probably paid one of those men at the Hot Spot."

Billy's mind raced through possibilities. He had already come to realize that Roy had been right: this was entirely different from bouncing in a biker bar. There, the trouble was right in front of him, in a contained space—his turf, really. Out here, the advantage was all on the opposition's side, and he had someone else to protect. He thought about trying to get word to his father, and quickly discarded the idea. Yes, he could overcome his pride, but not the logistical problems of getting to a phone unseen. Besides, two cops had already died trying to help them. The police were obviously not the answer. He continued pacing. "Well, we can't stay here," he finally concluded.

"I know," Melissa agreed.

Billy turned to Walter. "Is there another way out of here?"

"No. Just the one, unless you think you can find you way through twenty miles of swamp."

Billy glanced at Melissa and shook his head. "So what do we do?"

"We have to get you out of here at night. You still got that motorbike up by the store. I can help you get to it, but there's not much I can do after that."

"I couldn't ask you to help any more than you already have."

"Son, we haven't done anything but let you sleep on the floor."

Billy ran a hand through his hair and continued marching back and forth. He could feel the perilous taunting of his old life calling him back, as though it had mistakenly let him escape for a short while and would now reclaim its captive. He pushed that thought away, too. He'd rather die than return to that torture. If they got out of this—no, *when* they got out of this, things were going to be different. He and Melissa would make a better life, together. But right now he had to be careful. Everything was on the line, and his first priority was making sure Melissa did not get hurt.

Billy spun around at the sound of an outboard motor. He started to scoop Melissa up to pull her inside, when a man rounded the corner and waved at Walter. "It's okay. That's Mr. Brown," Walter said, gesturing to indicate that Billy could relax. The man pulled his boat onto the bank and ambled up to the house.

"Howdy," Walter called from his chair.

Mr. Brown tipped his cap. "Afternoon."

"Want a glass of tea, or a cup of coffee?" Mary offered.

"No, thank you. The missus wanted me to tell you folks she suspects the Burrows kid will try to bring those men out here…probably tonight."

"Yeah, we figured that. Come on up, and have a seat."

"I really can't. Got to get back to the bar. Had to close it to come out here, and I don't like leaving it closed any longer than I have to." He took a couple of steps back. "Oh, and the missus wanted me to apologize. Said she should have known better than to send that boy out here in the first place."

"You tell her not to worry about that no more."

Mr. Brown tipped his head toward Billy. "You'd better get her out of here tonight. Those men ain't playing games. They're flashing money around like there's no end. About six or seven of them, and they have guns. Be careful, son."

Billy nodded.

Mr. Brown again tipped his head and headed to his boat.

Walter called, "Thanks for coming out."

Mr. Brown waved his hand over his head without looking back. He stepped into his boat and left.

The sun was setting in the background, but there was still light enough to distinguish figures when Stephen saw the young man return to the area behind the store. He nudged Jay and nodded in the boy's direction.

Stephen caught the young man's eye after he had dropped a stringer of fish into a bucket of water and wiped his hands on his pants' legs. He motioned the boy over. He felt a deep satisfaction at having been right; there was always somebody like him in every little low-life town like this. The boy walked straight to the car. Stephen opened the rear door and got out to greet him.

"Stephen Pruit," he said extending his hand and flashing his warmest smile.

"Rick Burrows," the young man returned, clamping Stephen's hand in a firm grasp. "How can I help you?"

"We've been looking for a girl…"

"What's it worth to you?" Rick cut him off.

Stephen's smile grew bigger. "I like that. A man who gets right to the heart of the matter."

"How much?" Rick repeated.

"I confess, the girl is worth a lot to me. She's my wife."

Rick set his jaw and dug his heels in. "Two thousand!" he shouted. "I'll take you to her for two thousand dollars, and not a penny less."

"Two thousand!" Stephen repeated in mock horror. He shook his head as though reeling from the staggering amount, and whirled around to look at Jay. Jay gasped, threw his hands in the air, and walked away.

"Yes sir, two thousand and not a penny less!"

"Two thousand dollars. I don't know. I mean, she's important to me, but that's a lot of money." Stephen looked at the ground, rubbed the nape of his neck, and paced back and forth a bit. "How far away is she?"

"Far enough. You won't find her without me. But I can take you right to her." Rick's voice grew less confident. Stephen pulled at his chin and put a quizzical look on his face, as though weighing the money against the girl. Finally, he made a show of swallowing hard. "Okay, okay. I'll do it."

"I'll give you two hours to get the money together and I'll meet you right back here, deal?" Rick talked so fast his words ran over each other.

"Deal!" Stephen reached out to shake the boy's extended hand. "Two thousand it is," he said. "I just hope I can pull that much together in two hours." He could have given him the money right then and there, but thought better of pulling twelve thousand dollars out of his pocket, and counting off two.

"Well, if you want the girl, you'll just have to do it," Rick said with a swagger that made Stephen almost laugh. "I'll meet y'all here."

"Okay. Ya'll come back now, ya hear?"

Rick chuckled to himself as he walked away. If he had any idea he had just been insulted, he did not show it.

Stephen laughed to himself and got back in the car for the two-hour wait. He'd have time to watch a video and enjoy a few drinks.

CHAPTER 30

❦

By the time Billy helped Melissa down the stairs and out to Walter's boat, it was pitch dark. The only light came from an oil lamp, which cast gloomy shadows as the couple said their good-byes and left the house. Seconds later, the light was extinguished. Walter hobbled along behind the couple with his twelve-gauge pump-action shotgun. Mary remained in the doorway, her hands folded in prayer.

Billy got Melissa settled into the boat, sat beside her, and waited for Walter to shove off. Melissa held on tightly, as the small boat rocked unsteadily. "Everything's going to be all right," he whispered in her ear.

She nodded, but said nothing.

"I'll be waiting for you right here," Mary's voice called to Walter.

Stephen thought it best to drive around a bit to make Rick think they were desperately trying to gather the enormous amount of cash required for his services. Then he had the limo park off to the side, around a corner, so it wasn't visible from the store. After exactly two hours, Rick knocked on the window. Stephen got out.

"I got the money," he said, feigning a tone of excitement as though it had been a real challenge. He pulled four crisp $500.00 bills out of his pocket.

Rick licked his lips and extended his hand. "I'm ready when you are, but I want the money first."

Stephen handed him the money.

Rick looked at the slips of paper and frowned.

"Something wrong?" Stephen asked.

"No, I guess not. I just thought $2,000.00 would look bigger."

Stephen smiled, "Would you like me to give it to you in ones?"

"Can you?"

"No. That was supposed to be funny."

"Oh."

Stephen clapped his hands. "Well, let's get started."

Jay motioned and the other three men got out of the car. The driver remained ready behind the wheel. Rick started at being surrounded by so many men in suits, all armed except Stephen.

"You're not going to kill her, are you?" he asked nervously.

"Of course not," Stephen reassured him. "These men are here to protect her. We just want to make sure she gets home safely."

"Oh, okay. I'll go get the boat ready."

Rick headed toward the water while Stephen gathered his men around him for last-minute instructions. "Okay, remember: don't kill the freak, unless it's absolutely necessary. Just get him out of the way as quickly and quietly as possible. And make sure nothing happens to Melissa. She's no good to me dead."

Stephen led his men toward Rick's boat. As they neared the water, he stopped abruptly and held up his hand.

"Wait!" Stephen motioned to Rick to not start his motor, and waved the men back. "Hear that? Another boat's coming in. Everyone pull back and let it pass." Stephen led the group back to the car and watched as the shadowy boat emerged from the darkness. He could see that there were several people on board, but couldn't make out any faces or shapes. The boat stopped behind the store, almost out of sight. The darkness behind the small building made it even harder to see, but he could tell they were unloading something, probably their catch. Finally, a little old man hobbled around the edge of the building into the moonlight.

"That's him!" Rick whispered excitedly. "That's Walter, the guy she's staying with."

"You're sure?"

"Yeah, yeah! That's him!"

Stephen stepped out from around the side of the car. "Excuse me, sir," he called out pleasantly.

BOOM! Flames leapt from the barrel of Walter's shotgun. A barrage of small holes appeared in the front fender of the limo. All the men plowed in the gravel. The driver lunged from the car to hide behind the rear bumper. The clicking sound of the pump action echoed in the night as Walter loaded another round in the chamber.

"Wait a minute, wait a minute, don't shoot!" Stephen shouted.

BOOM! The passenger's side window shattered. The old man was on a rampage. The kick from the gun nearly knocked him off his feet. BOOM! More pellets splattered against the side of the car. BOOM!

BOOM! BOOM! He loaded another round into the chamber.

"Wait a minute!" Stephen screamed. His men had drawn their guns and were retreating to the safety of the darkness and whatever buildings or trees they could find to return the fire.

BOOM! The old man staggered back as more pellets splattered across the rear half of the car.

A motorcycle roared to life and took off in a blaze from the opposite side of the store. Stephen could make out his wife on the back. The driver had to be the freak. In his surprise, Stephen started to stand.

BOOM! Pellets from Walter's shotgun whizzed by his ears.

BOOM! BOOM! Several other people from the community started firing into the air. Rebel yells and shouts of confusion echoed throughout the small community as more guns joined in.

"Don't shoot that old bastard!" Stephen commanded his men. "These trigger-happy hicks are never going to let us out of here if you kill him."

Stephen crawled to the car on his belly and motioned for his men to follow. Within seconds the limo took off, slinging gravel behind as it departed. Stephen could see the shadowy image of the old man as another flame blazed from the shotgun. The rear window exploded. The car swerved, then straightened and took off after the motorcycle. The sound of gunfire quickly faded.

Within a few seconds they caught sight of the motorcycle. "Don't shoot!" Stephen commanded. "I don't want her hurt!"

The chase led them down Highland Road and onto Interstate Ten. "Stay on his tail. Don't let an inch get between us!" After a few minutes, the bike veered off the highway and headed into the city streets.

"Stay with them," Stephen commanded the driver. "Watch for cops," he spat over his shoulder to the men in the middle seats. "Stay with them, stay with them," he muttered under his breath.

The bike sped down several streets, skidding around corners at the last minute, and weaving between the old beer bottles and trash that littered the roads. At one point, it zipped through the space between two houses, both boarded up and bearing CONDEMNED signs, but still showing signs of life inside. "Go around the block! Catch up to them! Catch up to them!"

The limo streaked around the corner, all eyes searching every side street. "There they are!" one of the men in the back shouted. The driver slammed on the brakes, spun the car and streaked down a side street, careening around the next corner. The bike was there, but several blocks ahead of them. "Put your foot through the floor!" Stephen roared.

The bike made another sharp turn and the driver wiped out a mailbox trying to whip the limo around the corner fast enough. Finally, they came to a long stretch with no houses or street lamps.

The bike leapt forward and sped into the darkness, its motor screaming.

"Faster! Faster!" Stephen screamed.

The bike wobbled as the pavement changed to gravel. The narrow road emptied suddenly into a large parking lot next to a small factory. The bike made a circle as if to leave the way it had come, but the limo was rapidly closing that hole. Stephen almost laughed out loud as the bike skidded to a stop and the two figures ran stumbling toward the buildings hand-in-hand.

"Get them!" The men poured out of the limo almost before it came to a stop next to the two figures. Billy pulled Melissa behind him as they were quickly surrounded.

Stephen slid out of the car and strode deliberately over to the group. "Well, there you are. I've been looking all over for you!" he exclaimed as though he had just found his child in a crowded store.

Melissa stiffened at the sound of his voice. One of the men reached out to grab her, but Billy snatched his hand and turned, breaking the man's elbow at the joint. The man screamed and collapsed, hugging his arm close to his body. Billy squared off to face the rest.

"Now, now," Stephen chided. "No need to get ugly. Oops, no offense to you, of course," he added with a chuckle, nodding at Billy.

Billy's heart pounded. He instinctively knew he was out of his league, and just as instantly recognized that he could not win against all of them at once and still protect Melissa. Flight had been cut off. Rescue would not happen. His body made the decision before his mind could catch up. He lunged forward and punched the closest man, grabbed a handful of his hair and slammed his head against his knee. Another man was grabbing him by the shoulder. He turned on the third man with a looping punch as the second man fell to the ground. A fourth jumped on his back. Back on their feet, two of the others were hammering at him with their fists. Billy stumbled around, trying to dislodge the one on his back and ward off the ones in front. The rear man wrenched at his neck. He tripped and fell face down into the gravel. In short order, the three men had his legs and arms pinned down. He struggled for a few minutes, then his head took over and he lay still, breathing hard. The men dragged him to his feet. Stephen stepped up.

"Well, well," he cooed. "Looks like…"

Billy jerked a leg free and kicked him in the groin. Stephen clutched at himself and stumbled back. Billy stomped down on somebody's foot and fought free. He wrestled the man closest into a chokehold. He spun around to use his body as a shield, but something hard hit the back of his head. He lost his chokehold grip and the man broke free. Billy tried to regain his balance. Something else, harder, bigger, struck him squarely in the back of his head. He stumbled forward, blood streaming down his back and shoulders. He groaned and fell to his knees.

"Billy!" Melissa cried from the ground, where Stephen had thrown her. "Billy!"

Billy took another blow on the side of his head. He grabbed at the air, gasping. Blood coursed over his face.

A brick came at him. He threw out an arm to stop it, but missed. It hit him full in the face. He dropped to the ground.

"Billy!"

Melissa's voice sent a surge of adrenaline through his veins, and he struggled back to his feet. He took a wild swing, but the man bobbed away. The sheer weight of Billy's own arm caused him to stagger and fall. The men stepped in again and dragged him to his feet. He hung in their grip. "I'm sorry, Melissa," he whispered.

"Billy!" Melissa had made her way to her feet and Stephen grabbed her by the arm.

"I don't think so."

One of the men struck Billy across the forehead with the butt of his gun just as he struggled to sit up. Billy crashed back to the ground.

"Billy! Billy!" Melissa tore away from Stephen's grasp and rushed forward, she tripped over Billy and fell to the ground. She began feeling around for him. When she found him she threw her body across his and felt for his face.

"Melissa, I'm so sorry," he mumbled.

"Oh, God," she sobbed.

Stephen grabbed her hair and lifted her to her feet. He shoved her at Jay. "Hold this."

Billy was fading in and out of consciousness, his eyes rolling back in his head each time they closed. Stephen straddled his crumpled form, leaned over and slapped him. "Do you have any idea how much trouble you've caused me?" He stepped away, turned to wipe Billy's blood off his hand on Melissa's face, and gestured at the car. "Let's get out of here."

Billy forced open one eye and watched Jay put Melissa into the car. "Angel face," he said, barely above a whisper.

Melissa heard him. "I love you!" she cried back.

Jay slammed the door. Stephen and the rest of the men got in and the car took off, slinging gravel back at Billy.

Billy lay in a heap, blood seeping out of his wounds, and visions of the devil dancing and laughing with glee floating through his head. Finally, his eyes slid closed for the last time.

CHAPTER 31

"Hey buddy, are you all right?"

Billy didn't know how many times he had come to and lost consciousness since the car with his love had sped away. And he didn't care. He had failed utterly. His body was broken, his head felt like it would come apart if he moved it, and his love was gone. All his fault. At the sound of the stranger's voice, Billy pried his eyes open, but the sun was up and bright. He quickly let his lids drop again. He'd seen enough to know a man wearing a flannel shirt and carrying a lunch box was kneeling anxiously beside him.

Billy did not move. He barely had the strength to speak, and no desire at all to respond.

"You're alive! Thank God," the man said. "I'll call an ambulance."

"No."

"What?"

Billy gathered all his strength to reform the word. "No." He timidly tried filling his lungs. Surprisingly, they still worked. "I'll be fine," he mumbled. He took a deep breath and rolled to the right, and pushed himself to his knees. The stranger held his arms out, crossed, and Billy grabbed them and pulled himself to his feet. He stood there swaying for a moment, the stranger "spotting" him on either side. "Thanks," Billy half whispered, half gasped.

"Hey, man, take it easy now. You don't want to make things worse."

Billy barely held himself up as he looked around for the bike. Pain shot through his head with the movement. He took another deep breath and began to choke, until he swallowed a thick, gooey clot of blood stuck in his throat. He let the stranger help him stumble across the gravel toward the motorcycle. It was still where they had let it fall on its side when he and Melissa had run. He reached down to lift the bike.

"Hey, forget that," the workman said. "I'll get it." He set the bike upright. "You know, you're in no shape to drive this thing," he warned.

"Yeah, I know." Billy carefully swung his leg up to straddle the bike. He sat there panting. He had to hold his head very steady so his brains wouldn't leak out.

"Now, you hold on there," the workman said. "I can't let you try to do this. You wait right here. I'm going inside and call you an ambulance." He trotted away, then turned back. "You wait right there, now, ya hear?" He trotted to the chain-link security fence, inserted a key into the gate lock, and headed toward the closest building.

Billy carefully reached down, flipped the key, and revved the bike. Wincing against the pain and fighting to keep both eyes open, he drove slowly around the neighborhood looking for an entrance to the interstate. Once on, he headed south, driving slow, no more than 45 mph. Any faster, and he'd either lose control of the bike or his head would fall off his shoulders.

He knew he couldn't make New Orleans. He exited on Highland and headed back to Alligator Bayou. If he could just rest a few hours he'd be fine. Maybe, somehow, someway, he could find Melissa again and help her, as he had promised.

He had slowed to only a few miles per hour, but lost control of the bike when he turned onto the gravel road. It swerved, wobbled, and turned over. He lay on the side of the dirt road, too weak to pull himself back up. His wounds started bleeding again, the blood making gooey mud of the dust underneath his head.

Billy opened his eyes. Tree limbs were passing by overhead. His body swayed with the motion of some kind of vehicle. Boat? No. Maybe a car. No, it was open. A pickup truck? He faded out again. The next thing he knew, Mrs. Brown was wiping his face with a wet cloth. This time, he recognized the familiar rocking of a boat.

Neither Walter nor Mary had slept a wink all night. They had walked the floor worrying about the young couple. It was almost 6:30 in the morning when they heard the motor. They rushed to the porch. Mr. Brown's boat was coming toward the house. Mrs. Brown was waving a handkerchief in the air like a signal. The elderly couple hurried to the bank where the boat would dock. When it was close enough, Walter pulled it onto the bank. He saw Billy.

"Is he dead?" the old man asked softly.

Mrs. Brown shook her head. "No. But I didn't know if we should take him to the hospital, or what. After all of the shooting last night, I didn't want to get him in any more trouble. Don't really know what's going on, don't want to make matters worse, so I've second-guessed myself every step of the way."

Mr. Brown jumped out of the boat and helped Walter pull it up far enough on the bank to hold it in place.

"Well, by God. They tried to kill him!" Walter exclaimed. "He must have lost a lot of blood." He carefully lifted one of Billy's eyelids. The eye flickered and closed.

Mary cupped her hands over her mouth. "Oh Jesus, Jesus, help us Lord."

Mr. Brown and Walter made a stretcher out of a thick blanket and moved Billy to the couch in the living room of the small cabin. Mary gathered cloths and fresh water, and cleaned the wounds gently but thoroughly, dressing each one with ointment. She wrapped Billy's head in a bandage made from an old white sheet while Walter and Mr. Brown cut off his bloody clothes and helped make him more comfortable. Mrs. Brown dribbled a little water on his mouth, waited for him to lick his lips, then dribbled some more.

"Well, I think he got a little water, but he needs a lot more." Mrs. Brown said as Walter and Mary were seeing her and Mr. Brown off. "We'll come by tomorrow to check on him. Try to get as much liquid into him as you can."

Walter stood over Mary for a while, watching her wipe Billy's face and drip water onto his dry, cracked lips. Some he swallowed, some just ran down the side of his face. At length, Walter went out on the porch, sat in his rocker, and stared at the floor.

Inside, Mary's tears trickled down her old, worn cheeks and fell to mingle with the tiny droplets of water she coaxed into Billy's mouth. She would stay there all day and all night, if necessary. It gave her something to do with her hands while she pleaded with God for his life.

CHAPTER 32

Melissa remained silent and stony-faced all the way back to New Orleans. She sat in the rear, which had been perfunctorily swept out at the first opportunity, because, Stephen claimed, he did not want her delicate skin to get cut by the broken glass. She had moved as far away from him as possible, but couldn't get away from Jay, who had handcuffed his wrist to hers. The melancholy sound of the wind whistling through the broken-out windows provided a perfect match to the ache in her heart.

"It's not going to do you any good to sit there and sulk about it," Stephen growled after a while. "He's dead."

Her eyes started to fill with tears, but she fiercely fought them off. She wouldn't sully her love's heroic efforts with weakness. She no longer cared what Stephen might do to her; she would not let him have what he wanted. He had taken Billy away from her, and she would suffer whatever torture and pain she must to keep him from succeeding. If money was all he wanted, she would die herself before she let him get it.

She felt the car slow down and make several turns. Stephen told the driver to go through the drive-through.

"Do you want something to eat?" he asked.

She didn't answer.

"You want something to eat?" he asked again, louder and more demanding.

She turned her head away.

"Melissa, stop acting childish. You knew how this was going to turn out all along. Now, enough is enough. You belong at home, with me. I'm your husband, after all. Now, answer me! Do you want something to eat?"

Melissa took a deep breath, let it out, and remained silent. Stephen grumbled a string of profanities at her, then asked Jay what he wanted and gave the order to the driver. A few minutes later, the car resumed its normal motion.

The aroma of hot food throughout the back of the car made Melissa sick to her stomach, but it also reminded her of the aromatic smell of Mary's wonderful breakfast, which, in turn, quickly brought thoughts of her last night with Billy, followed by the sound of his body hitting the gravel and dying voice whispering her name into the wind. Despite herself, the tears trailed down her face. She wept silently, her mind unable to focus on anything more than the void in her chest, which, for a brief while, had been bursting with joy.

The car bounced, turned, and made several stops before finally coming to a halt at the mansion gate. She recognized the familiar turns of the long driveway up to the house.

"Take her to my office," Stephen commanded.

Jay tugged on their attached wrists. She pulled back. "Come on now," he said. "You know this is only going to make things worse." He pulled on the handcuffs and grabbed her other arm as well. "She doesn't want to get out," he yelled out the door.

"It doesn't matter what she wants!" Stephen shouted back. "Take her to my office!"

Jay grabbed a handful of her hair, dragged her from the car, and let her fall onto the cement drive. The car door slammed shut behind her.

"Are you going to get up, or do I have to drag you all the way across the walk and up the stairs?"

Melissa wobbled to her feet with one hand, her other held high above her head the entire time by the linked chain. Jay pulled on her shackle, someone grabbed her free arm and she was led into the house and up the stairs. The familiar smells and feel of the house seemed to pierce her already broken heart. With every step, it felt more and more as though she had never left, and instead had just awakened from the most beautiful dream. She stumbled, and the two men lifted her up the rest of the stairs, letting her feet drag behind. She wouldn't help them. She had no desire to move the slightest muscle. She was surprised her heart continued to beat. No life was left in it.

The men dropped her into the same chair she had sat in countless times before. She heard the click of metal—the other end of her handcuff had been moved to the chair arm. She could still feel both men somewhere to either side of her. Presently, she heard the door open and Stephen enter the room. His footsteps made the same trotting, arrogant sound as always. When she first met him, she had thought he walked with presence. Now she heard only vanity and conceit.

He walked around the desk, flopped down in his chair and prop his feet on the desk. The chair squeaked as he leaned back. She waited.

"You know what's coming, Melissa?" he asked after a long moment.

She said nothing.

"Answer me! Do you know what is coming?" he demanded.

She neither moved nor spoke.

"Melissa," he said, irritation rising in his voice. "Why do you want to make this worse than it already is? You know I'm going to get what I want, anyway. If you make me angry, you'll only pay for it more. Is that what you want?"

She was no longer listening. She was back in her own private hell with Satan her jailer. She would find no escape from the tyrannical rule of her greedy overlord this time, no shining knight to come to her rescue this time. The one person brave enough to try lay beaten to death for his effort.

"Melissa!" Stephen shouted at full volume.

She jumped at his outburst. She raised her head as though she could look at him.

"What?"

"I just want to get a few things straight. Then you can go to your room and rest. I'm about to make a call to Anderson and arrange a meeting between myself, you, him, and a friend of his. He's going to have a few papers for you to sign regarding the house insurance and several other domestic issues. Do you understand?"

She nodded, knowing full well he lied.

"Very well, go to your room and clean up, get some rest and I'll send you some dinner later."

She lifted her manacled arm. A moment later, she felt it being released. She stood and walked slowly to the door, out into the hall and down the passageway to her room. Only when she had carefully closed her own door and made her way to the bed did she allow herself the release of flinging herself onto her pillow and letting the tears fall freely. "Why, God?" she implored. "Why dangle the promise of happiness and then crush any chance of getting it?"

She wept bitterly for the rest of the afternoon.

CHAPTER 33

Around three the following afternoon Billy began to stir. He had been unconscious for over 24 hours, with no sign of life other than his faint, but growing heartbeat. He had moaned once, and once his hand had twitched as though he were having a bad dream.

Mary had sat watch over him the entire time with a tenderness that came naturally to her. She had slept on the floor beside his couch, eaten her breakfast within arms' reach, and even had Walter take her place while she bathed.

This was, in many ways, her chance to make things up to her son. Every time she looked at Billy lying on the couch, she saw her son lying wounded in the mud, his life ebbing away, all alone. She had felt so guilty for not being there, she'd hardly slept the first year after his death.

Billy moaned, flinched and began to thrash about. Mary wiped the cold sweat from his forehead. "Take it easy, baby," she soothed. "You're just having a bad dream. Take it easy. I'm here."

Billy opened his eyes with a start. He half expected to see a fist coming at him, or the barrel of a gun. Instead, a big, toothless grin set in a wrinkled, worried face hovered just above him. He steeled himself and tried to sit up. Mary placed a hand on his chest. "Easy now," she whispered. "Easy. It's gonna be all right, baby. Here, try to swallow a little, that's right. Now just rest. We're all praying for you, it'll be all right."

Billy lay back, panting. He tried to gather his thoughts, place himself and where he was. Gradually, the mists cleared and he remembered. Melissa's image filled his mind; shuddering, tears began to stream down his face. Each icy heartbeat drove the pure, unadulterated pain into his every cell. "It's all right baby," Mary's soothing voice said again. "Everything's gonna be all right. Have another little swallow."

He drifted away once more, but this time only into a deep sleep, filled with nightmares of Melissa being tortured and calling his name. He struggled to get to her, but his hands and feet were bond tightly in place no matter how much he strained. The scene went on and on, over and over, seemingly for hours. When he woke again, the room was pitch black.

Pain shot through his head with the quick cracking snap of a bolt of lighting in a cold night sky when he tried to lift his shoulders off the couch. Spasms thundered through his chest and arms body. His mind fogged over.

"Just lie still, baby. Don't try to move," Mary warned softly. She disappeared for a moment, returning a moment later with a new cool, wet cloth. She squeezed some water into his mouth. He licked his lips and closed his eyes.

In his semi-conscious state, he could feel Mary's warm, nurturing presence beside him throughout the night. Every time he approached consciousness or stirred, the cool cloth or a tender hand touched his face, a few drops of water fell onto his dry, swollen tongue. He fought to stay there, to not lapse back into the terrifying world of restless nightmares, where painful memories turned into monsters, demons, and worse. The bad dreams chased him back up Mary's tender touch, which relaxed him and sent him plummeting down again.

He went back and forth throughout the night. He woke to sunshine streaming through the front windows and the smell of cooking food, which made him nauseous. He rolled his head slightly and opened his eyes. Mary's face crinkled into a big smile. His mouth was dry, and his tongue felt too large to fit inside.

"Morning, baby."

"Thirsty," Billy mumbled.

Mary dribbled a little water onto his tongue.

"More…please," he whispered.

"Bring me a glass of that water," she called to Walter, who was over by the wood stove fixing breakfast. Walter grabbed the pump handle, filled a large container with water, and handed Mary a glass. She cradled Billy's head and lifted it enough to place the edge of the glass to his lips, then slowly tilted it until the water trickled into his mouth. Billy swallowed as much as he could before he began to choke and cough. Lightening bolted through his head. Mary set the glass aside and gently lowered his head.

"Want some more?" she asked.

Billy formed the word "Yes" with his lips, although no sound came out. Mary waited a few seconds, then repeated the process. "Tiny sips, baby, tiny sips. You haven't had nothing but driblets for days."

Slowly, in fits and starts, he managed to drink half the glass. Mary's face glowed as she lay his head on the pillow.

"You think you could drink a little chicken broth?"

Billy moved his head. "No."

"Son, you're not going to be able to help that girl if you don't eat and get your strength back," Walter's voice said from somewhere beyond his field of vision.

Billy carefully moved his head. Walter had brought his rocking chair in, and was watching him from the other side of the room, his face set in a mixture of fierceness and concern. Billy clenched his teeth and pushed himself up on one elbow. "Okay," he mouthed, his voice lost somewhere inside the pain.

Mary held a cupful of warm chicken broth under his chin, and Billy sipped at it with a straw until he reached bottom. He lay back for a moment to catch his breath, then lifted himself again, nodded slightly at Mary, and drank another cupful. The broth hurt going down and made his stomach feel queasy, but he forced down three full cups, resting between each one. Finally, he mustered all the strength he could summon and tried to raise himself all the way up.

"No, no, honey, just rest," Mary pleaded.

"Mary, leave the boy alone now," Walter said from his observation point. "He's got a job to do."

Mary cupped her hands to her mouth, her arms pulled tightly to her chest. Her eyes grew wide with concern, but she remained silent.

Billy set his jaw, braced his mind and pushed himself to an upright position. He swayed there for several seconds before falling back to the couch. Mary's hands were already there to ease him down. He floated away to the sound of her voice whispering a prayer in his ear.

CHAPTER 34

❀

Stephen answered his portable phone on the first ring.

"Hello."

"Stephen Pruit, please."

"This is he. How can I help you?"

"Mr. Pruit, David DeBello here," the voice said cheerfully. "Glad to finally talk to you myself again."

"Yeah, it's about time," Stephen answered with a snort of impatience. "I've had a hell of a time keeping my wife contained for the last six days. I didn't expect to have to wait on your convenience!"

"Sorry about that," David said in his thick, fake southern. "I've been at the Governor's Mansion all week. But I'm back now, and I understand you're ready to move on that project your brother and I discussed a few weeks ago."

"I've been ready for a stinking week," Stephen snapped.

"Well, as I said, I was at the Governors Mansion. I'm certainly not going to apologize for that."

Stephen drew a long breath. "All right. What now?"

"I'd like to meet with you and your brother in my office sometime this afternoon, to go over what I have in mind for you. I think you'll be pleased."

"I'm not taking her off the grounds again! Last time it cost me almost a hundred million dollars!"

"Oh, I don't need the girl yet. I just need a couple of hours to go over the paperwork and make sure everyone understands what's going to happen."

Stephen's throat tightened. "You do know my wife is not willing to go along with any of this, don't you?"

"Yes, yes," David said quickly. "But I don't think this is really the proper place to discuss it, is it? We'll deal with whatever problems arise during the negotiations, on the spot—so to speak."

Stephen almost started to protest, until he caught the gist of what David was saying. Then he settled back in his chair and relaxed.

"I understand," he said.

"Good. Then that's settled. What time can you be here?" David asked crisply.

"It'd be better all around if you came out here later today. I'll make sure Anderson is here, and we'll set aside an hour or so for discussion. Then as soon as everyone is in agreement, we can bring her in and close the deal."

"I usually don't do business outside of my office, Mr. Pruit," David admonished, "but for you, I'll make an exception," he added hurriedly. "It's 10:00. How does four this afternoon sound to you?"

"That'll work," Stephen said gleefully. "I'll have Anderson here and…"

"Why not just have Anderson pick me up? It'll be easier than me trying to find the place."

"Fine, fine. I'll tell him to have you here at four." Stephen smiled at the wall. "I look forward to meeting you."

"The pleasure, sir, will be all mine, I'm sure."

Stephen could hear the smile in his voice. It was a trick for building trust Stephen knew well.

CHAPTER 35

Billy walked down the steps in front of Walter's cabin while Mary stood in the doorway, crying. She had pleaded with him to stay a little longer to ensure his full recovery, but he refused. He had already spent almost a full week getting his strength back, working his muscles back to life, and planning his course of action. If this had been an ordinary situation, he might have taken another few weeks, maybe even a month or two, to return to full health. But this was no ordinary situation.

Mary had wrapped his head in fresh bandages, but the clean dressings didn't change the hatred in his eyes—hatred, Walter had explained to her, that could be almost as powerful as love. Combine the two and nothing was impossible. Billy knew Melissa was still alive—he could feel it. He longed for her with every fiber of his body and soul, and his peaceful surroundings only served to amplify the rage and anguish boiling inside him and the sheer desperation that dominated all his thoughts. They would have justice!

Walter was waiting for him at the foot of the stairs. Billy took the last two steps with a leap. Pain shot through his head when he landed on the ground with both feet, but he made his face smile rather than grimace. Walter understood why he had to go, and go now; Mary, on the other hand, would hold there him at gunpoint if he so much as a hinted that he was still in pain.

He and Walter waved good-bye to Mary from the edge of the boat. Walter climbed in first and took his seat. Billy shoved the craft into the water and stumbled, nearly falling, before he regained his balance and took his seat.

"You better not let that girl see you stagger around," Walter warned. "She'll tie us both to the couch." Walter smiled and waved to Mary again. "Wave to let her know you all right."

Billy quickly smiled and waved to Mary, who meekly waved back. Once the boat had turned away from the house, Billy grabbed hold of the sides with both hands. Walter yanked on the old pull-cord motor until it struggled to life, spitting and sputtering. He flipped the switch to put the motor in forward gear and took off. He turned and waved one last time to his wife before the cabin disappeared behind the trees.

"I never been good at lying to her," Walter mumbled. "She knows you're not all right."

"I'll be fine."

"I know you're still hurt. But I also know you have to go. Just be careful."

Billy nodded.

Within a few moments, they rounded the corner to Alligator Bayou. Billy jumped out and pulled the boat securely onto the bank. Walter made his way to the ground with Billy's help, and the two proceeded to the front of the store. Rounding the corner, they came face-to-face with Richard Burrows, who gasped and mad a beeline for his boat. Paddling away under the glaring eyes of both betrayed men, he started his heavy-duty boat motor within seconds and was gone.

Billy found the motorcycle propped on the side of the building, where Mrs. Brown had ordered it placed. He pushed it to a little dirt clearing in front of the store and straddled it. The screen door creaked open. Mrs. Brown stood on the edge of the porch, wringing her hands.

"Those marks must have got there when you wrecked," she said, pointing to the side of the gas tank. "I had them put it back over there for safekeeping."

"Thank you," Billy said. "I really do appreciate all your hospitality."

"We'll be praying for you, child." Mrs. Brown chewed her lip, nodded, and went back into the store.

"What's wrong with her?"

"She's just worried about you, son," Walter said. "We all are. People just show it differently, that's all." He placed a wrinkled hand on Billy's shoulder. "Now you take care of yourself, son."

"I will."

"And you come back and see us sometime. You can help me check the trout lines." Walter attempted one of his hysterical laughs, but it came out cracked. He stopped abruptly.

"I'd love to," Billy assured him.

"Those are dangerous men. I seen people like 'em before. Don't care 'bout nothing but money. Don't let them get you, son."

Billy hugged the frail old man. "Thank you."

He started the bike and took off. A few minutes later he turned south onto Interstate Ten, headed back toward New Orleans, Melissa, and whatever he had to do to be reunited with her forever.

CHAPTER 36

❦

David DeBello settled into the back of the waiting limo with Anderson at 3:45. "Good to see you again," he said. "How was your week?"

"Not bad," Anderson replied cheerfully, shaking David's extended hand. "Not bad at all. How about yours?"

"Great. The Governor is always a very gracious host. I'll have to introduce you to him sometime."

Anderson kept his face straight, but his heart jumped at the suggestion of meeting the Governor.

David interrupted his reverie. "Have you thought about our little chat?"

"Yes. It's about all I have thought about."

"Well, what do you say?"

Anderson nodded. "Let's do it."

"Outstanding!"

They talked no more as the car made its way to the mansion. By the time they stopped at the gate, it was 4:45. One of the guards logged the visitors in while the other pushed the intercom button to announce them. He waited a minute and pushed it again.

"What?" Stephen's voice snapped through the small speaker.

"Mr. Anderson Pruit and Mr. David DeBello are here to see you, sir."

"It's about time! Send them in!"

Overhearing Stephen's frustration from the back seat, David and Anderson exchanged disdainful looks. The car made the twisting journey up the long driveway, with the guard dogs following them a short way, then losing interest. The driver held the car door open for them, then led them to the den, where Stephen was on his second drink of the afternoon.

"Mr. Pruit and Mr. DeBello."

Stephen came around the end of the couch. "Stephen Pruit," he said, extending his hand and offering a tight, thin smile.

"David DeBello," David returned. "Glad to finally meet you."

"Yeah," Stephen answered dryly. "I thought you would be ten feet tall, the way Anderson carries on about you."

"No, only five-foot-six and a half," David said, his smile turning plastic.

"Why don't we have a seat over here and get started?"

"Show me what you've got," Stephen said after they were seated.

"Very well." David opened his briefcase and spent the next hour-and-a-half describing the myriad phases and levels of his plan for Stephen's financial future, always careful to include "with a small percentage as my fee, of course" at the end of every phase. He spoke in broad, complex legal terms which specifically avoided hinting at any part of the side deal he and Anderson had previously discussed. Every now and then, Stephen glanced at his brother, who seemed to be listening intently and would give his a reassuring nod or "thumbs up." Finally, Stephen was sufficiently confused to be impressed.

"Outstanding," he said, exhaling with satisfaction. "Let me get Melissa and we'll close the deal."

Stephen left the room. David and Anderson exchanged a fleeting glance, then quickly looked away.

CHAPTER 37

As Billy approached the city it suddenly dawned on him that he needed a gun. Given enough time, he knew he could get one from one of the customers at the Hot Spot, but time was the one thing he lacked. He still had most of the money James had given him. Surely he could pick up a gun somewhere. As the city grew nearer, his nervous energy increased. The pain in his head had subsided now, reduced by the ever growing adrenaline in his blood, empowering him like a nuclear reactor with its infinitely hot core searing his rational thought, and leaving in its wake only one purpose.

He saw the city, only a few miles ahead now, clearly visible in the darkening horizon. Nothing could stop what was about to happen—for better or for worse. He tried to convince himself over and over that everything would work out in the end, but he knew it could go either way. He would not kid himself about his chances of success. Without Melissa, his life meant nothing to him. In his heart and mind he was ready to die, and he knew that gave him a huge advantage over his weaker opponent.

He passed the New Orleans airport and stopped the bike at a run down pawnshop. He propped the bike on its kickstand and went inside. The store clerk showed him the various handguns, most out of his price range. But, he did find several he could afford. The clerk, an older balding man, wore horn-rimmed glasses, and dressed in seventies' style disco clothing, complete with orange polyester bell-bottoms. His voice was deep and scratchy from too many years of drinking hard liquor, and he spoke slowly as though searching for each word.

"How about this one?"

"Let me see it," Billy said, as he reached out for the scratched up old revolver.

The clerk unlocked the glass cabinet, pulled the gun from its resting place, and handed it to across the counter Billy.

"How much?"

"One hundred and fifty dollars," the clerk answered flatly.

"What about a box of bullets?"

"I only have a small box left; it's eighteen bucks."

Billy eyed the cheap, used gun—designed to look like a more expensive brand, but without the logo. He worked the cylinder around a few times and tried to act like he knew more about the weapon than he actually did.

"It's a fine little handgun," the clerk said.

"I'll take it," Billy announced, "and a box of bullets."

"Okay," the clerk said. He grabbed a slip of paper from under the counter and slid it across the glass top to Billy. "Fill that out, please."

"What's that for?" Billy asked.

"It's for your checkout," the clerk said. "You have to pass the checkout before you can get a handgun."

"How long does that take?"

"Not too long, just need your personal information, and you driver's license."

"I don't have a drivers license."

"Then you don't have a gun, either."

"Why do I need a license to get a gun?"

"It's the law." The clerk sniffled and scratched his head. "The new federal background check.

"I need this now."

"Not going to happen. I can hold it for you until you get a license," the clerk said in a slow sleepy-sounding voice.

"Is there anything you can do?" Billy asked, trying to calm himself to appear less desperate.

"Nope. If you want the gun, you fill out the paper and show me some ID. Otherwise leave."

Billy knew that he was making the clerk nervous with his urgent need for a gun. He did not want to cause any trouble and end up in jail. He knew, by experience, it would take Roy a day or so to get him out, and he just could not spare the time.

"Never mind," Billy said as he turned and walked away from the counter. He got back on the bike and headed for the French Quarter. After a few minutes he parked in front of the Hot Spot, got off the bike and walked in.

The place looked the same as he had left it. The bar teamed with the same type of crowd, the same type of girls, the same smoke, and the same type of music. In the short time he had been gone he'd forgotten just how sleazy the place was. James spotted him and bolted to toward the door.

"Are you all right?" he asked pointing to the bandages wrapped around Billy's head.

"Fine," Billy said. "Can I borrow your pistol?"

"Wow, wait a minute now," James said, "Let me get Roy over here. He has been worried about you."

Billy walked past James and, with no further conversation, went to his room and closed the door behind him. He clicked on the light and picked up his sword. The urgency he had felt days ago now raged completely out of control. It consumed his every thought, and filled his heart with a driving force as powerful as a raging waterfall. He could wait no longer. Billy knelt and stood the sword before himself like a knight of the Crusades.

He bowed his head, "Help me-Jesus-please help me," he whispered. He closed his eyes, took a few deep breaths, then rose, and bolted for the door. He passed James on the way out—already on the phone looking for Roy. Billy walked past the bar grimly, his eyes narrowed, his vision focused.

Outside he hopped on the bike and took off, following the general directions Melissa had given him during one of their conversations. She had told him the house was on the road by itself, and that it was impossible to miss.

The time had come, and within the next few hours he would know his fate.

CHAPTER 38

Melissa sat on the floor beside her bed, with tears flowing down her bruised face. She had slipped back into the same hell from which she thought she had escaped. She was still sore and hurting from the beating Stephen had given her the night she choked him, but the pain from the cuts and abrasions were minimal compared to the pain that raged in her heart. She picked up a snifter Stephen had left on the nightstand. He had actually taken a break from beating her long enough to have a drink.

She held the glass by the stem and smashed the thin, top-half against the nightstand. She felt the top of the glass for the sharpest piece and, when she did not feel what she looked for, she patted the floor around her. Her fingers found the perfect piece of glass; large, oval shaped, and sharp. She leaned her head back against the bed and thought of Billy. Her mental image saw him gallant, like a mighty knight who fought to his death to protect his fair lady.

The tears flowed down her face in a steady stream, and the pain in her heart surged. What lay ahead terrified her, but she would see Billy again, and she prayed that it wouldn't take long. She remembered hearing stories of deathbed experiences, where people told of how loved ones waited to embrace the newly departed. She wondered if she would see Billy, or her father. What if they were watching her now, waiting for her to make the final commitment so they could be together forever? In the stories she had heard, people with defects were whole on the other side. Perhaps she would look into her father's eyes for the first time, and see the love in Billy's eyes she felt coming from his heart. Would there really be angels? Jesus? God?

She buried herself in thoughts of rapture and delight, as she tried to build her courage. Paradise awaited her on the other side. It would take only a few brave seconds and she would be there. Never to be separated from her loved ones again. Never to be abused and beaten by a cruel, cold-blooded snake like Stephen. Never again would she endure rape. No more humiliation. No more pain. Eternal bliss with her loved ones forevermore.

She slipped the sharp glass across her wrist, and felt the warm, sticky blood flow. The cut did not hurt nearly as much as she had thought it would. She placed the glass in her teeth and drew her other wrist across it. The blood spurted across her face, and she wiped it off on her upper sleeve. She dropped her hands by her side, tilted her head against the bed, closed her eyes, and thought of Billy waiting for her with outstretched arms. Waiting to hold her. Waiting to love her. A warm, peaceful feeling came over her, and she smiled.

CHAPTER 39

Roy had continued to worry about Billy and wondered if Stephen Pruit had taken his threat as seriously as he should have. He had meant every word. Given a choice he would rather have Billy alive than Stephen Pruit dead, but it had left his hands when Billy left. He could only wait and hope for the best.

He and G-man had worked out a plan, in case things went in the wrong direction and he had to kill Pruit. G-man arranged for duty near the dispatcher, and see to it that friendlies were sent to the scene with predetermined reports. No one would question them, and even if they, did everyone would remain safe so long as they all stuck to the story. The chosen cops, all friends of Donny Hebert and Clyde Robicheaux, despised cop killers. They all agreed on the best way to handle a cop killer.

Roy took a bite from his muffoletta, and a drink from a cold beer. He sat at a small po-boy shop on the outskirts of New Orleans, in Slidell—a favorite of his, since early in his career. They had always provided the cops with free meals, and some of the best the food in the state.

Roy had just lifted the sandwich to his watering mouth to take a bite when his beeper went off. He set the food down and pressed a button on the side of the beeper to display the number, then rushed to the phone. He knew the call had to do with Billy. It always had to do with Billy when James called.

Roy jumped behind the shop's counter and picked up the phone without asking. He and the shop proprietor had been friends for over fifteen years, and had long since brushed aside asking permission to use the phone. He dialed the number.

"Hello." James answered with a quick nervous voice.

"Yeah, this is Roy, What you got?" Roy asked excitedly.

"He was here about ten minutes ago. I tried to call your house and, when I couldn't get you there, I beeped you."

"Yeah," Roy said.

"Anyway," James continued, "he was here. He got his sword from his room and left. He wanted my gun, but I told him he needed to wait for you. I think he's going after the girl. She wasn't with him, and he's very upset. He had bandages around his head too."

The beat of Roy's heart increased. "Call John Smith, at home. Tell him to stand by for my call. He'll know what you're talking about."

"What if I can't reach him?"

"Then beep him."

Roy gave G-man's home phone and beeper numbers to James, then waved to the shop proprietor and ran to his car. In a few short seconds he was speeding down the interstate on his way to the Pruit mansion. He was quite a bit further from the house than Billy, and he hoped he could get there in time.

CHAPTER 40

❀

Stephen tried to open the door to Melissa's room and found it blocked from inside. He knocked on the door and called her name. He knocked again. Still no answer.

"Melissa, this game is getting old," he threatened. "Open the door."

Nothing happened. Stephen slammed against the wooden barrier. He slammed into it again; nothing happened. He slammed into it the third time, and the door flung open with a bang sending small splinters through the air. He reached for the light switch. It had grown totally dark outside and the windows provided no illumination. When the light came on he panicked. Melissa was sitting on the floor beside her bed, with blood all around her. She jumped when he shouted, so he knew she was still alive, but just how stable he could not even guess.

He rushed to her side and examined her wounds. The cuts were deep. She had definitely tried to kill herself, but had cut the wrists from side to side, and the blood was already starting to clot. She had lost a lot but, not enough to kill her—or to keep her from signing the contract.

Stephen searched around the room and found two hand towels. He wrapped them tightly around her wrists and tied them with shoestrings.

He patted her on the cheek. "Melissa honey, are you all right."

She stirred and moaned, "I'm sleepy."

"Just wake up for a little while. I've got a few things to go over with you, then you can sleep all you want."

She opened her eyes and tried to wrestle away, but he slapped her hard across the face.

"Damn it, Melissa, be still," he shouted.

He lifted her over his shoulders and carried her from the room and down the steps.

"We need to make this quick," he shouted.

Billy passed a large iron gate with the name Pruit written in gold across it. He slowed the bike down and turned around.

As they approached the living room Melissa could hear people scrambling around the room. She knew this was the day Stephen and Anderson had planned, and the day she had tried to avoid. Stephen dropped her in a chair, and she swayed back and forth, but did not fall over.

"Melissa, this is David, he has some papers for you to sign," Stephen said as he wiped blood from her face.

David stood nervous, and opened his briefcase, as he cast glances from Melissa to Stephen to Anderson. He pulled the contracts from the leather carrier, and placed them on the coffee table.

"Mrs. Pruit," he said, as though they were conducting business in formal fashion. "If you would please sign the paper on the line. It is raised so you can feel where to put your signature."

Melissa sat still.

"Sign the paper, Melissa." Stephen said sternly.

David placed the contract on his brief case and set it in her lap.

"If you reach out, Mrs. Pruit, you will find the contract just a few inches from where your hand is now."

Melissa sat without moving, fully aware now of what was going on. She bowed her head and clenched her teeth.

"Sign the paper, Melissa!" Stephen commanded.

She remained motionless. Stephen slapped her behind the head and she lunged forward knocking the briefcase to the floor. Melissa refused to move.

Stephen stood behind her and kicked her in the back of the head with the heel of his shoe. Her head bounced forward limply, as the force sent her sprawling to the floor on top of the briefcase. She knew she was in for the beating of her life. She had failed at killing herself, and now she had to face the thing she so wanted to avoid. She sniffled and began a sorrowful sobbing, like a small child alone and afraid. She lay helpless on the cold floor, limp and unmoving, feeling the threatening presence of the three men towering over her.

CHAPTER 41

Billy parked the motorcycle about a hundred yards from the gate of the Pruit mansion. He placed the sword on his back and walked toward the gate. Energy now raged through his body and he could no longer feel any of his injuries. He watched the lights from the little guardhouse grow closer and wondered how he'd get inside.

He approached the guardhouse casually and walked up to the guards with a smile and a wave.

"How's it going?" he asked.

The two guards looked puzzled like they thought he was crazy. One of them shrugged his shoulders, and responded, "Fine," he answered.

"Yeah, I'm here to see Mrs. Pruit," he said.

The guards looked at each other curiously. Then a glint of recognition crossed their faces.

"Oh, you're the freak," the guard to the right said. "They told me about you." He turned to the other guard, "He's ugly as hell, ain't he?"

The guard to the left noticed the handle of the sword, and laughed.

"You've got to be out of your mind," he said. "Is that a sword?"

One of them reached for his pistol, but in a flash the sword came alive in it's master's hands and sliced open his throat. Then in one quick continued motion it chopped the right hand off the other, obeying its master without question, and performing flawlessly. The one-handed guard clenched his nub to his chest and tried to wrap it in his shirt. Gurgling sounds came from his dying comrade, and at that moment he felt more respect for that sword that he would have for an atomic warhead.

"Which one of these buttons opens the gate?" Billy asked.

The guard sat in shock trying to stop the blood from pouring out of the open end of his arm. Billy slapped him on the side of the head.

"Which one of these open to gate?" he repeated sharply.

"The green one," the guard gasped.

Billy pushed the green button, stepped over the dead body of the guard, and disappeared into the night.

Stephen knelt beside Melissa and again slapped her behind the head. He withdrew his hand coated with blood from where he had kicked her.

"SIGN—THE—PAPER—MELISSA—NOW."

Melissa did not move.

Stephen grabbed a handful of her hair and, with his right hand pulled her head back sharply, with his left he placed the briefcase and contract before her and picked up the pen. He folded the fingers of her right hand around the pen and placed it to the proper place on the paper smearing blood across the document.

"Sign…the…paper!" he shouted, jerking her head with each word.

She gasped for air, and a grunting sound came from her throat as she tried to breathe. Stephen slapped her once more, then stood and kicked her on the side of the face. Her weak body turned completely over, and he grabbed her hair and jerked her to a sitting position. She let out a painful cry. He placed the briefcase in her lap and made her hold the pen with limp fingers.

The intercom buzzed.

"Sign the paper Melissa, or I will cut you to pieces!"

"We can't use this paper, Stephen. Its got blood all over it." Anderson spoke with more courage than normal.

"I don't care. She is going to sign it anyway." Stephen shouted. "She will learn not to disobey me."

Anderson looked at David and nodded an affirmation. David nodded back slightly and both turned their gaze to the floor.

Stephen went on in a tirade, focused on a goal that would bring no results. "Sign," he screamed.

The intercom buzzed.

Stephen slapped her across the face several more times, and kicked her in the stomach. She doubled over crying in pain and moaned like a dying animal. He had broken her spirit and she knew it. The pain in her midsection was unbearable. She started shaking violently all over. Her tiny shoulders jerked, and she cried out loud. Limp, hopeless, and defeated.

The intercom buzzed two or three times in quick succession.

Melissa's trembling hand held the pen. She knew if she would just sign, it would be over at least for now.

Stephen slapped her again and her weeping became heavier. She was defeated. Stephen had won, and there was nothing she could do about it.

The intercom buzzed again and Stephen slapped at it and shouted, "What?"

"He's here sir!" The voice was thin and weak.

"What are you talking about? Who's here?"

"Billy!"

Melissa gasped so hard it caused her body to jerk. She threw the pen across the room and let her tears flow forth. Her hero had come for her, even death could not keep him from her.

"Go kill that freak," Stephen shouted to Jay.

Jay walked quickly from the room.

"You're the one who's going to die, Stephen!" Melissa shouted through her tears. "You're going to die."

"Shut up!" he shouted.

"He's going to kill you for what you've done to me!" The tears flowed down her face, and ran along the creases made by her smile.

Stephen stomped from the room.

As Billy made his way across the lawn he heard dogs running toward him and in a flash, they charged at him like hellhounds through the darkness. The first one jumped at him and fell to the ground in two pieces. The second animal lunged and again Billy slashed with the sword. The dog yelped, and crumbled to the ground, not dead, but he would fight no longer. Billy moved on through the darkness toward the glow of the house. Three men ran from the front door, and he knew the guard must have warned them. He cursed himself for not killing the man when he had the chance. He placed himself flatly against the wall of the house next to a corner.

Soon, one of the men rounded corner. One quick slice and the man fell dead with a grunt. Another man appeared from directly behind the first. He grabbed for his pistol, but died before he could use it. The man made little sound as his lifeless body fell to the ground. Billy picked up the pistol and placed it in his belt. He put his foot on the dead man's face and worked his sword free with both hands. Then he went to look for the third man.

Stephen returned to the room with a twelve-gauge shotgun-a single shot that he used for skeet shooting. He broke the barrel down, and placed a shell in the chamber, and then tapped Melissa on the head with the gun barrel.

"Sign, Melissa," he said, surprisingly calm, "or I'm going to kill you."

Melissa threw the briefcase across the floor. The papers scattered in the air and came floating back down like huge flat snowflakes. She jumped to her feet and made her way quickly toward the door, but Stephen was on her in a flash. He pushed her next to the wall and placed the barrel of the gun to the back of her head.

"Get the papers!" he screamed at Anderson.

While Anderson gathered the contract, a gunshot echoed from outside.

"There goes your boyfriend!" Stephen shouted as he nudged the back of her head with the gun barrel.

Anderson stood beside Melissa and held the contract against the wall. He placed the pen in her hand and moved it to the right spot on the page.

"Sign, Melissa." Stephen shoved the gun in the back of her head, forcing her head to bump against the wall. "Your boyfriend is dead, and you lose. Sign the paper."

He shoved the gun to her head again and caused her forehead to slam against the wall. She swung her hand behind her head and slapped the gun barrel. It moved only a few inches, and discharged. A mist of Anderson's blood and brains filled the air behind him. The gun had gone off at point-blank range, only an inch from his face. His body hit the floor, as chunks of his bloody brain slid down the wall.

David jumped up and tried to wipe the fine mist of blood from his own face, but it only smeared. He ran from the room. "Don't call me, and don't get me involved in this."

Stephen threw the gun, and stood almost in shock. In the confusion Melissa bolted through the door and out into the yard. Stephen grabbed a steel poker from the fireplace and ran after her in a fit of rage.

Melissa screamed for Billy as she ran down the hill toward the trees. She ran as fast as she could, but she knew Stephen was gaining on her. In her weakened state she merely stumbled along, but she fought with every ounce of strength she could muster.

"You bitch!" he screamed. "I'm going to cave your head in!"

Melissa called Billy's name again and began to panic when he did not answer her call. She ran wildly to the bottom of the hill to hide in the trees. She stretched her hands forward and ran until she came upon the first tree, where she slowed down and tried to make her way into the woods. She could hear Stephen only a few feet behind her, and tried to run faster but, tripped and fell. She instinctively covered her head with her arms, waiting for the first strike.

Stephen slowed from a run to a walk as he approached the fallen girl.

"I told you!" He raised the steel rod over his head and glared down at his helpless victim. He grit his teeth and prepared to strike, when a crashing right hand sent him to the ground with a grunt.

"Billy?" Melissa managed to ask.

"It's me, Angel Face." Billy tossed the sword to the side.

Stephen regained his feet and charged, but in an instant Billy grabbed the back of his head and slammed his head into a tree. Stephen staggered and fell. Billy pulled him to his feet and slapped him like a child. Stephen swung wildly at him, and Billy simply leaned to the side and punched him square in the face. Stephen fell back against Billy's sword and jumped to his feet with the blade in his hands. The two squared off, Stephen nervous and afraid, Billy calm and confident. He swung the blade down toward Billy's head. Billy twisted to the side, grabbed the handle of the sword, and jerked Stephen forward. The razor edge of the blade lay next to Stephen's neck as Billy looked him in the eye.

"You ready to die?" he whispered. Billy pulled the sword so that it sliced into Stephen's jugular.

Blood arced into the air. Stephen touched the side of his neck then looked at his blood-soaked hand. He grabbed the side of his neck, as shock hit him. He sat against the tree with a stunned look in his eyes.

He covered the cut with both hands trying to stop the steady flow of blood that oozed between his fingers.

Sirens sounded in the distance, growing closer.

Billy knelt beside Melissa. She jumped when he touched her.

"It's okay. It's me," he said softly, and tenderly brushed her hair from her bruised and battered face.

She collapsed in his arms. "Oh Billy, I thought you were dead!"

He kissed her gently on the forehead. "No. I told you I would protect you."

Tears welled up in her eyes and she pressed her face against Billy's chest. The agony that she had endured over the last week vanished in an instant. She was once again in the arms of her love.

"What about Stephen?" she asked.

Billy looked eye to eye with Stephen Pruit. "He's dead."

Stephen's mouth opened as though he was trying to say something. He looked wildly around, and tried again to stop life from escaping through his wound.

Several patrol cars screeched to a stop at the front of the house, and Roy bolted from around the corner. Billy helped Melissa to her feet and picked up his sword. The two of them walked halfway up the hill. Melissa stumbled weakly, and Billy picked her up in his arms. She laid her head on his shoulder and placed her arms around his neck. Billy held her tightly and walked up the hill toward Roy and the glowing light of the house.

0-595-25005-X